Cassidy's worst fears were being realized.

"Now," she said, eyeing the stranger. "Suppose you tell me what you're doing here, Mr. . . .uh, you never told me your last name."

He returned her frank stare and cleared his throat. "It concerns the advertisement I placed outside the general store."

Clapping a hand to her cheek, Cassidy opened her mouth wide in horror. This was the wife hunter? Why would a man as handsome as he need to advertise for a wife?

His eyes narrowed as he observed her reaction. "Is there a problem, Mrs. Sinclair? You did inquire about the ad, correct?"

"*Miss* Sinclair," she corrected. "You posted it?"

"We didn't exactly get off to a good start, did we. . .?"

Irrational anger boiled within Cassidy. "I should say we did not get off to a good start. Would you please explain to me what you were doing cooking bacon at my fire?"

He opened his mouth, but Cassidy gave him no chance to speak. Humiliation loosened her tongue and a torrent of words spewed from her lips. "Do you think just because I answered your ad you have a right to come right in and take over? Are you planning to move right into the wagon, too?"

She ignored his blink of surprise and continued, the words spilling from her lips like a rain shower. "If you think I'm the kind of woman who'd—"

He held up his hand. "Miss Sinclair, please let me explain myself."

TRACEY VICTORIA BATEMAN lives in Missouri with her family that includes a husband who is a prison guard, one daughter, three sons, a Husky dog who would like to believe he is human, and a guinea pig who seems to think he is a dog. When not focusing on the enjoyable role of wife and mother, Tracey loves to read, cook, and play piano. She is also very involved in the music department at her church. *Darling Cassidy* is her first published work of fiction—the fulfillment of a long-held dream.

Darling Cassidy

Tracey Victoria Bateman

Heartsong Presents

A note from the author:
*I love to hear from my readers! You may correspond with me
by writing:* **Tracey Victoria Bateman
Author Relations
PO Box 719
Uhrichsville, OH 44683**

ISBN 1-58660-171-7

DARLING CASSIDY

All scripture quotations, unless otherwise noted, are taken from
the King James Version of the Bible.

All of the characters and events in this book are fictitious. Any
resemblance to actual persons, living or dead, or to actual events
is purely coincidental.

Cover illustration by Jocelyne Bouchard.

PRINTED IN THE U.S.A.

one

The mid-April wind whipped at Cassidy Sinclair's black muslin skirt as she stood outside the roughly hewn dry-goods store, scanning the notices on the wall. Her gaze rested on a poster written in bold, black letters:

WANTED:
**Woman of marriageable age and status.
Must love children.**

An advertisement for a wife?

Cassidy read it again to be sure.

What sort of man posted an ad for a wife? Her mouth curved into a small, ironic smile at the hope rising in her heart. On the other hand, what sort of woman considered accepting the offer?

The desperate kind of woman with a child to raise, she admitted.

With a heavy sigh, she peered closer at the notice. Smaller letters declared: If interested, inquire within.

"Aunt Cass?"

"What is it, Em?" she asked absently, keeping her gaze fixed on the post.

Her niece yanked insistently at her skirt. "Aunt Cass!"

Frustrated, Cassidy glanced down, hard pressed to keep the irritation from her voice. "What is it, Honey?"

Emily rolled her large green eyes to the side. "Don't look," she whispered, with all the dramatics only a seven year old could muster, "but that man over there is watching you."

5

Cassidy couldn't resist an amused smile at the child's vivid imaginings. "What man?"

Emily's face grew red, and she stomped her foot. A frown creased her brow. "I'm serious this time," she hissed. "There *is* a man watching you. He could be an outlaw."

"Oh, honestly, Em," Cassidy said, shifting her gaze to the possible scoundrel, if for no other reason than to prove to Emily that, if there were a man looking in their direction, his interests most certainly weren't focused on them.

Spying the man in question, Cassidy drew a sharp breath. Wavy, coal-black hair topped his head, and the shadow of a beard covered his face, giving him a rugged, outdoorsy appearance. He wore a light-blue shirt with sleeves rolled mid-way up muscular, deeply-tanned arms. Cassidy's heart did a little flip-flop. He was easily the most handsome man she had ever seen.

Her gaze caught his, and his eyebrows shot up.

Shame filled her at her brazen appraisal of a perfect stranger. And that particular stranger, she admitted, was about as close to perfect as anyone could get.

Stop it! she ordered herself, but she couldn't keep her heart from thundering in her chest.

She held her breath as his glance swept her from head to toe and back again. When he lifted his gaze to meet hers, his cobalt blue eyes held a look of undeniable appreciation.

He flashed her a devastating, but obviously amused, grin, and Cassidy suddenly came to her senses. With a prim lift of her chin, she shot the stranger a reproving look and draped her arm around Emily's shoulders. "Come. Let's go inside."

"Do you think he's really an outlaw?" Emily asked in a loud whisper. Cassidy cast a quick glance back to the stranger, wondering if he had heard. He smiled, showing straight white teeth. With a chuckle, he bowed gracefully, his eyes shifting to Emily, who blushed and giggled at the broad wink he sent her.

"Come, Emily," Cassidy said again more firmly, steering the child toward the door of the general store.

"But he's coming right toward us. It wouldn't be polite to walk away!"

Pretending not to hear her niece's plea for propriety, Cassidy pushed the girl through the doorway and slipped quickly inside, hoping he wouldn't follow.

Unable to resist the urge to venture a little peek outside, Cassidy's breath caught in her throat as the handsome man stepped up to the store window and looked in. Catching her eye, he smiled, tipped his hat, then turned and strode away.

"Somethin' I kin hep you wit', little lady?"

Cassidy whirled around, then stepped back instinctively as a giant with a bushy black beard walked around the counter and towered over her.

She cleared her throat. "Yes. I. . .um. . .I wondered about that notice outside."

"Which un ya mean?" He spit a stream of tobacco juice, missing the spittoon in the corner by a full foot.

With great effort, Cassidy fought to contain the nausea overwhelming her stomach. "The one about a man needing a wife," she said, dropping her voice a notch and glancing cautiously at the other customers.

His booming laughter filled the dusty little store, and Cassidy had a strong urge to reach up and yank his beard to hush him up.

"Well, Ma'am, I never thought we'd git a taker so fast-like. Jus' put that up today."

Relief filled Cassidy. No one else had applied, then.

Listen to yourself—applying to be a wife!

Suddenly aware that she was the object of several curious stares, Cassidy felt the humiliation down to her toes. Spinning on her heel, she turned to remove herself from the most embarrassing moment of her life. But she stopped short as her gaze rested on Emily.

Thick, carrot-orange curls twisted into tight braids hung down the little girl's back. Her bonnet, which Cassidy tried to no avail to keep on the girl's head, dangled from the loosely tied laces around her neck. Her tender, fair skin had far too many freckles as it was without exposing it to the sun's burning rays, but Emily hated the confinement of a bonnet and rarely kept it on.

Cassidy's heart sank as Emily's wistful gaze rested upon a bowl filled with brown hen eggs. She knew exactly how her niece felt. It seemed like forever since they'd tasted much more than beans and sourdough biscuits. Emily wouldn't ask for them. She knew the money had disappeared long ago, spent on supplies and unforseen repairs to the wagon. Eggs were a luxury they simply couldn't afford, no matter how their mouths might water for a change of menu.

Cassidy was so weary of doing without the things they'd taken for granted before William had died, leaving a mound of debt and his young daughter for her to raise.

As she observed the longing in Emily's face, Cassidy came to a decision. Her niece would not do without, even if she, Cassidy Sinclair, had to marry a stranger to assure it.

She squared her shoulders and faced the bear of a man. "The notice said to inquire within. Now, if you have any information, please pass it along." Crossing her arms firmly across her chest, Cassidy met his gaze, eyes blazing.

Shifting his stance, he folded his massive arms and grinned. "So you wanna be a wife, eh?"

Resentment coursed through Cassidy at the ill-mannered question. "Just tell me how one should go about responding to the notice."

Wondering if she was due another rude remark from the storekeeper, Cassidy held her breath while he assessed her. But when he spoke, all teasing had vanished. "You come in with the wagon train, today?"

"Yes, Sir."

"How long ya be stayin'?"

"Indefinitely. Emily and I won't be continuing with the others."

The man thought for a moment, stroking his matted beard.

"Just gimme yer name, and I'll pass it along to the feller whut put it up."

"All right, then," she replied with a decisive nod. "I'm Cassidy Sinclair, and this is my niece, Emily."

Emily gave him a wide, gap-toothed grin. "Pleased to make your acquaintance," she said with a small curtsy, then stretched out a tiny, freckled hand to the giant.

With a twinkle in his eyes, the man wiped his hand on his dirty buckskin shirt and accepted hers. "Likewise, little missy." He turned back to Cassidy. "One other thing, Ma'am."

"Yes?"

"Where kin the feller find ya?"

"Oh." Cassidy hadn't thought of that. "I suppose I'll stay with the wagon train until they pull out day after tomorrow. But if the man who posted the notice doesn't show up by then, we'll find a boardinghouse somewhere."

He nodded. "I'll tell 'im. Now, anythin' else I kin do for you and the little missy?"

"No, thank you. We'll be going now. Come along, Em."

With a last, longing glance at the bowl of eggs, Emily followed her aunt.

"Ma'am?"

Cassidy stopped just before reaching the door. She turned back to the trader. "Yes?"

He cleared his throat and shifted his huge, moccasin-clad feet. "Um, I'd like to give you a welcoming gift."

She raised an eyebrow. "Whatever for? You don't even know us."

He glanced at Emily, his expression softening considerably. "Fact is, we don' see many red-headed little girls with freckles, an' I'd like to give ya a gift jus' fer the pleasure of havin' her in my store."

Emily blushed and hid behind Cassidy's skirts.

A rare show of timidity, Cassidy thought wryly.

He thrust the basket containing at least a dozen eggs into her hands. "There, that's the gift I'd like to give ya," he said, looking quickly away.

Emily's eyes widened. Cassidy drew in her breath, and her mouth watered as she stared with longing at the treasure. But reason returned, and she shook her head. She didn't know this man. What might he expect as payment?

Regretfully, she pushed the basket back into his large hands.

"Aunt Cass," Emily groaned.

"You're very kind, I'm sure," Cassidy said to the bewildered man. "But we can't accept gifts from strangers. Good day."

She whirled around and slipped swiftly out the door with Emily in tow.

Once outside she looked about the small town, pushing back the anxiety filling her at answering the advertisement. What other choice did she have? Her legs ached from walking all day, looking for a suitable position. From laundress to seamstress, there was simply nothing available, and she couldn't stay in town permanently without a means of support.

Oh, how she longed for the life she'd had before William had died. When cholera claimed Cassidy's widowed brother a few months earlier, she'd taken his daughter, Emily, to raise as her own. Cassidy's brother hadn't been the most practical man in the world, and he left the Missouri farm deeply in debt. Within a couple months of his death, creditors forced her to sell off the farm and equipment to pay the bills, and Cassidy and Emily had no choice but to leave.

Not long before the sale, an excited neighbor spoke of going west, sharing his dreams of a new land where anyone could prosper. His excitement lit a fire in Cassidy, and she decided that she and Emily needed a new start. So, with as much courage as she could muster and the small amount of cash left after her brother's bills were paid, she packed up their meager belongings and set off for Independence, Missouri, praying she would find a wagon master willing to accept her into his westbound train. By some miracle she found a train heading to Santa Fe. The wagon master, Lewis

Cross, a red-faced little man with a kind heart lying beneath his gruff exterior, agreed to let her join with one provision. "As long as you don't hold up my train," he'd said.

To Cassidy's dismay, only three weeks passed before the problems started. Her rickety wagon suffered a broken wheel caused by deep ruts in the well-worn trail. A man from the wagon behind Cassidy's offered to fix it for her, but Mr. Cross grumbled about the hours the train was forced to stop.

She had hoped her troubles were over but could have wept when, merely one week later, the axle split in two, once more causing a delay while repairs were made. Mr. Cross took her aside and gently suggested that she quit the trail in Council Grove and find a domestic position.

Assessing her options, Cassidy had to admit that the wagon master was right. A thirty-five-year-old spinster with a niece to raise would never make it to Santa Fe alone. So here she was, five weeks after leaving her Missouri home, trying desperately to find a suitable way to make a living for herself and Emily. With all her options exhausted, there was nothing to do but go back to the wagon and pray someone would come to marry her.

Cassidy slowly came to consciousness, then sat up with a start. The sun no longer filtered in through the seams of the worn canvas as it had when she'd crawled into the wagon. A pounding headache earlier in the day had sent her to her bed, but she had only meant to lie down for a little while. Poor Emily must be famished.

The fragrance of coffee and bacon from somewhere in the wagon train wafted into the covered wagon, making her empty stomach grumble. For a moment, she wished she had more to give Emily for supper than the ever-present beans and sourdough biscuits.

With a sigh, she pushed back the quilts. Still seated on the bed, she grabbed her boots and slipped them on, then, reaching forward, laced them up.

From outside the wagon, she heard Emily giggle. With a slight frown, Cassidy peeked outside. A gasp escaped her lips. The man she had seen outside the general store earlier, now stood over her cast-iron skillet, frying bacon. He looked large and out of place performing the feminine task, and she had the urge to shoo him away and take over. Subconsciously, she smoothed back her hair, then opened the flap wider.

Emily turned to her with a grin and skipped to the wagon. " 'Evening, Aunt Cass," she said, brightly. "You sure slept a long time. Your head feelin' better?"

"Yes, Dear," Cassidy replied with a smile, "much better."

The man straightened and strode to the wagon. "Hello. We didn't have a proper introduction earlier." His velvety voice nearly stopped her heart. "I'm Dell."

She accepted his proffered hand and gave it a firm shake.

Looking at their clasped hands, his eyebrows shot up in surprise. She loosened her grip and inwardly cringed. Why couldn't she be dainty like other women?

"Let me help you down," he offered.

Reluctantly, she slid into his arms. The soap-scented smell of him made her pulse quicken, and she pushed quickly away from his arms—too quickly.

He stumbled backward, grabbing at her to keep from falling. Cassidy lost her footing, and they both fell to the hard ground in a tangle of long arms and legs.

"Get off of me," Cassidy spat.

Emily laughed uproariously.

"I'm trying, Woman," he grunted. "Be still so I can get up."

She stopped struggling while he disentangled himself from her. Once on his feet, he held out a hand. Warily, Cassidy allowed him to help her up. He brushed at her back, but she stepped away.

"Please," she said, holding up both hands, palms forward. "Stop."

"Only trying to brush off the dust," he replied, a crooked grin teasing the corners of his mouth.

She raised her chin, trying to hang on to her shredded dignity. "I–I can brush off my own dust."

"Now, let's start over, shall we?" he said.

"Fine," said Cassidy breathlessly. "I'm Cassidy Sinclair and this is my niece—"

"Emily," he finished, winking at the little girl. "I know. We've already met."

Emily smiled, her face turning pink.

Cassidy scowled at their camaraderie. Emily was far too easily influenced for her own good. But just as she was about to send the little girl to the wagon while she tried to figure out what this man was doing cooking at her fire, he suddenly frowned and sniffed the air.

Cassidy raised a curious eyebrow just as the acrid smell of smoke reached her nostrils.

"The bacon—" He slapped his thigh and took two strides toward the fire. Grabbing the skillet, he let out a yowl and jerked his hand back.

"Here, let me." With surprising calm, Cassidy lifted the end of her skirt and grasped the hot handle. The pan sizzled as she thrust it into the basin of cool water. "Now," she said, eyeing the stranger. "Suppose you tell me what you're doing here, Mr. . . .uh, you never told me your last name."

He returned her frank stare and cleared his throat. "It concerns the advertisement I placed outside the general store."

Clapping a hand to her cheek, Cassidy opened her mouth wide in horror. This was the wife hunter? Why would a man as handsome as he need to advertise for a wife?

His eyes narrowed as he observed her reaction. "Is there a problem, Mrs. Sinclair? You did inquire about the ad, correct?"

"*Miss* Sinclair," she corrected. "You posted it?"

"We didn't exactly get off to a good start, did we?" He gave Emily a sly wink, causing her to giggle again.

What power did this man have over her niece?

"Em, go wait inside the wagon, please," she said, irritation edging her voice.

"Oh, Aunt Cass, I always miss the fun," Emily complained. Nevertheless, she stalked off to do as she'd been told.

Irrational anger boiled within Cassidy. "I should say we did not get off to a good start. Would you please explain to me what you were doing cooking bacon at my fire?"

He opened his mouth, but Cassidy gave him no chance to speak. Humiliation loosened her tongue and a torrent of words spewed from her lips. "Do you think just because I answered your ad you have a right to come right in and take over? Are you planning to move right into the wagon, too?"

She ignored his blink of surprise and continued, the words spilling from her lips like a rain shower. "If you think I'm the kind of woman who'd—"

He held up his hand. "Miss Sinclair, please let me explain myself."

Cassidy's racing heart settled a little at his soothing voice. "Fine," she said. "Start by explaining where the bacon— which you burnt—came from, and why you were cooking it in the first place."

He lifted a brow and twisted his lips into a smirk. "Well, I hated to invite myself to dinner without bringing the meat. Didn't have time to snag a deer. As to whether or not I move into the wagon," he said with a drawl, observing her with lazy eyes. "Now that remains to be seen."

She felt herself blush all the way to her hairline. "Your manners are insufferable, as I observed with the boldness of your stare this morning." She stamped her foot. "And stop looking at me that way!"

"I apologize if my admiration offends you, Miss Sinclair. But if you'll pardon me for saying so—and I wouldn't have brought it up if you hadn't first—I was simply returning a stare from you."

A gasp escaped her mouth. "Sir, you may turn around and go back the way you came. Considering your boorish manners, it's no wonder you have to advertise for a wife."

"Aunt Cass!" cried Emily from the wagon.

An inkling of regret passed over Cassidy's heart, and she wished she could snatch the words back. After all, if he took her at her word and walked away, where would she and Emily go?

Dell's square jaw tightened, and his eyes glittered like sapphires. "You think I'm looking for a wife?"

"Well, aren't you?" Cassidy swallowed hard as embarrassment flooded her. "The advertisement indicated marriage."

He observed her coolly. "I represent Mr. Wendell St. John III. Unfortunately, my employer's business keeps him too busy to attend to such things as meeting suitable women. So, he sent me instead. You seem to be the only candidate."

A strange sense of disappointment filled Cassidy. "You don't want to get married, then, Mr. . . .?"

"Michaels. Dell Michaels. Let's just say I want to find my own wife." With a businesslike air, he cleared his throat and produced a folded slip of paper from his shirt pocket. "This is a contract of sorts, stating that you agree to marry Mr. St. John, or—"

"Now wait just a minute—"

He held up a silencing hand. "Mr. St. John will outfit the rest of your journey," he said with a cursory glance over the worn-out wagon, "beginning with a new wagon. He will also provide material for a suitable trousseau. And I'm sure we can find something for your niece as well."

Cassidy glanced at her shabby dress and worn-out shoes and felt ashamed. "Mr. Michaels, please. I haven't said I'd go."

"Of course not. No decent woman would agree to such a marriage without further details, which I will provide if you'll stop interrupting."

Cassidy bristled but held her tongue.

"The contract in question is simply this: once you arrive at the ranch—"

"Mr. St. John is a rancher?" She'd only known farmers.

"Yes." He gave her a stern glance, silencing her. "Once you arrive at the ranch, if you find that Mr. St. John doesn't meet your expectations, you may work as his housekeeper. Or if you prefer, you'll be provided with transportation to wherever you choose to go." He paused. "Well? What do you say?"

"Oh, may I speak now?" she asked, sarcasm dripping from her lips.

With a light-hearted chuckle, he handed her the contract. "You may."

"Where is this ranch, anyway?"

"Southwest of here."

"It's in Kansas, then?"

Dell nodded.

"I'll have to think about this—and pray about it." She scanned the contract. It seemed to be in order. Still, she had to be sure God was behind this. Enough miseries occurred in the world when people jumped into things just because an idea sounded good.

His eyes held a glint of admiration. "The wagon train will probably be pulling out tomorrow or the next day. With all the Indian trouble, recently, I'd like to go with them as far as we can. If you can give me your answer early in the morning, we can sign the contract and pick up supplies. I'll have to clear it with the wagon master, but I don't think there'll be a problem."

"Fine. I will give you an answer then, Mr. Michaels."

"Well. . ." He glanced at the charred skillet. "Sorry about the. . .um, bacon. There's more in a crate over there. Enjoy it with my compliments." He lifted a large hand of farewell toward Emily, who peeked out of the opening in the wagon canvas.

Cassidy drew a breath as his gaze shifted to hers. "Until tomorrow, Miss Sinclair." He placed his hat atop his head and mounted his roan mare. With a final glance toward Cassidy he rode away.

❧

Cassidy thrashed about on the straw mattress, trying to get comfortable enough to fall asleep. Finally, she sat up and shrugged into her dressing gown. Yanking back the canvas flap, she stepped down from the wagon. A cool gust of wind blew across her clammy body, drawing a sigh from her lips. Her mind conjured up the face of Dell Michaels. If only he were the one seeking a wife instead of Mr. St. John. But she wasn't that lucky. Oh she'd had the dreams of a handsome beau sweeping her off her feet, just like all young girls. But beautiful girls got the handsome beaus, and young women like Cassidy sat like a wild flower among roses, never invited to dances or socials.

Perhaps if she had traveled west sooner she might have had a better chance at marriage. She had heard women were a rarity in the West—especially single women. Well, she was definitely single. For now anyway.

*Lord, is this Your plan for Emily and me? Mr. St. John is a stranger to us, but You've known him since You formed him in his mother's womb. Prepare us for each other, Lord. And maybe. . .*No, it was too silly to even ask.

Cassidy lifted her chin and looked into the night sky. The moon shone down on the camp, and a smattering of stars dotted a vast expanse, making Cassidy feel very small in the scheme of things. She remained outside until long after the others had doused their fires and retired to their own wagons. A sense of longing sent an ache across her heart as she heard the hoot of an owl calling to its mate. Everything in nature had a place to belong. Except her.

Still filled with a sense of melancholy, she returned to the wagon and laid down next to Emily. With a yawn, she closed her eyes. *And maybe, Lord, maybe I can even fall in love.* She drifted to sleep with images of a dark-haired man with brilliant blue eyes invading her dreams.

two

Dell scanned the wagons camped outside of town until he spied Cassidy standing over her cooking fire. She brushed a strand of hair, the color of ground ginger, from her face, then dabbed at her forehead with the edge of her apron. His heart stirred. *You're a lucky man, Wendell St. John.*

One thing he knew already: Cassidy Sinclair was quite a woman. Strong and solidly built, she stood a head taller than most of the women he knew. A prairie wife had to be tough and work hard. If a man was fortunate, he found a wife who stirred his blood as well. . .one like Cassidy.

As he approached her wagon, the aroma of smoked bacon wafting his way pulled him from his reverie.

"Good morning, Mr. Michaels," Emily greeted him with a wide grin as he dismounted.

"Good morning." He gently tugged a red braid, then his gaze riveted to Cassidy. " 'Morning, Miss Sinclair."

"Mr. Michaels." She inclined her head. "Are you hungry? Emily and I were just about to eat breakfast."

The rumble in the pit of his stomach served as a reminder that he had left his hotel room without food. "As a matter of fact, I'm starving." He strode to the fire and peeked into the skillet. Cassidy gave him a good-humored smile but said nothing.

"Ah, so this is how you fry bacon," he said, smacking his forehead with the palm of his hand.

Emily giggled. "What do you have there, Mr. Michaels?" she asked, indicating a small basket he held.

"Emily, don't be rude," Cassidy admonished.

The little girl scowled. "Sorry," she muttered, but she kept her wide curious eyes on the basket.

Dell struggled to suppress a grin. "Jasper, over at the general store, asked me to give these to you," he said, extending the basket toward Cassidy. "He said you wouldn't take them yesterday."

"Eggs! Aunt Cass, can we please have them now?"

A fleeting look of uncertainty passed over Cassidy's face, then she nodded, reaching for the basket.

"Will you join us, Mr. Michaels?"

"Please, call me Dell."

Cassidy tilted her head to one side. Lifting the crispy bacon from the skillet, she slid it onto a platter. "Dell, then. Do you want some breakfast?"

He admired the woman's disposition. As he'd discovered, she wasn't one to hold back. "I don't want to put you two ladies out." He sent Emily a sly wink. "Emily, here, is eyeing those eggs like a hungry fox."

"I'll share." Emily tried to give him a wink of her own, but her attempt produced a tight blink instead.

He chuckled. "There, you have it. If she's sharing, I'm staying."

"Good. You'd better start calling me Cassidy if you're going to eat at our breakfast table." She glanced at the quilt spread over the grass. "Well, our breakfast anyway." Turning back to the skillet, she cracked open the eggs one by one.

Dell's heart lurched. She was adaptable. That was for sure. He'd only known this woman for a day, but he was finding more and more to admire.

"Cassidy is an unusual name," he said. "I don't believe I've ever heard it before."

"It was my mother's maiden name."

"Lovely," he murmured keeping his voice low and even. His heart warmed as a modest blush rose to her cheeks.

Emily danced circles around the small campsite, arms stretched wide. "I haven't eaten eggs in years. I can't wait!"

"Think she's exaggerating just a little?" Cassidy glanced in his direction with a wry smile at her niece's antics.

Dell threw back his head and laughed.

Cassidy released a small, wistful sigh as she removed the eggs from the skillet and placed them on a platter. "It's amazing to me, now, what we took for granted living on my brother's farm. We had chickens and cows—all the eggs we could eat and milk we could drink."

"We have plenty of chickens and cows at the ranch," Dell said. "Little Emily, here, can have as many eggs as she can eat."

Cassidy's eyebrows lifted. "You live on Mr. St. John's ranch, too?"

Dell blinked, then stared. He cleared his throat. "Yeah, I have my own quarters."

"Are there many hands living there?"

"Only the foreman. . .me because I don't have a family. All the other hands live on nearby farms."

"Oh."

Emily plopped herself onto the ground and crossed her legs. Her eyes were wide with anticipation as Cassidy handed her a tin plate.

Dell followed her example and sat on the earthen floor beside her. With an indulgent smile playing at the corners of her lips, Cassidy handed him a plate, as well.

"Now, Emily," he said, glancing sideways at the little girl. "I'll show you the best way to eat one of these."

He moved his fork toward the perfectly round yellow center.

"Mr. Michaels, wait!" Emily shouted.

With a start, Dell dropped his fork. "What's wrong?"

"We haven't thanked the Lord yet."

He glanced up at Cassidy. Red-faced, she covered her mouth but couldn't conceal her amusement. Rather than embarrassing him, the action pleased Dell beyond words.

"Well," he said, in what he hoped was a dignified tone. "Let's hurry and thank the Almighty then, 'cause I surely am grateful for this breakfast."

They bowed their heads, and Cassidy said the blessing.

Dell studied their reverent faces and, for a fleeting moment, a longing rose within him. Though whether the longing stemmed from a need for faith in his numbed heart, or for the closeness of family, he wasn't sure.

"Amen," Cassidy murmured. When she looked up, her gaze found his and locked.

"Amen," Emily echoed and grabbed her fork. "I'm ready now."

Dell tried to respond, but lost in Cassidy's eyes, he found it impossible. His throat constricted and all he could do was stare.

Emily tugged at his shirt sleeve. "Mr. Michaels," she said. "It's okay for you to show me the best way to eat an egg now. Aunt Cass is done praying."

Cassidy shifted her gaze to Emily. The spell was broken.

"Yes. What is the best way?" she asked.

He cleared his throat and turned his attention to the little girl. "Well, you take your fork in one hand and your biscuit in the other." He grinned at his captive audience. "Stick the fork in the yolk and real quick-like sop it up with the biscuit."

Emily followed his example. "Mmmm, it is good this way."

Cassidy handed her a linen napkin. "Wipe your chin, Honey."

They laughed and chatted over breakfast. When the meal was over, Dell grabbed his dirty plate and a towel and followed Cassidy to the washtub.

"Why, Mr. Michaels—"

"Dell," he insisted.

"Whatever you say, Dell." She grabbed the towel from his hands. "No man is going to wash dishes in my kitchen."

"May I sit and talk to you while you work, then?"

She hesitated a moment, and he held his breath, afraid she might refuse.

"I suppose that'll be all right."

He sat on a crate and watched her hands move deftly from one dish to another. How long had it been since he'd watched a woman at work? Impatiently, he pushed back the painful memories trying to invade his mind. Now wasn't the time to think about the past.

Cassidy gave him a curious look. "Is something the matter?"

"No." His voice was sharper than he intended, and he softened it before his next words. "But I have quite a bit to do today—depending upon your decision, of course. Are you coming with me?" He held his breath, awaiting her answer.

Cassidy's jade green eyes stared frankly behind bristly lashes. "Emily and I are alone now, and if Mr. St. John is offering us a home, I don't see how I can refuse."

Relief washed over him. "Fine. I'll make the necessary arrangements."

"How long will it take to reach the ranch?" Cassidy asked.

She sounded weary and Dell's gaze traveled over her face. Dark shadows smudged the spaces below her eyes. The trail was hard for anyone; but he couldn't imagine what it had been like for a woman alone with a child to care for. Especially with her pitifully inadequate provisions. All that was over, now. He would make sure she never did without again.

"We'll stay with the wagon train for about two weeks. Then we'll turn off and travel another two days until we reach the ranch."

A frown darkened her face.

"What's wrong?"

"Two days with no chaperone? What will the neighbors think of me?"

Dell started to laugh but stopped, realizing by her wide-eyed stare that she was serious.

"Well," he said, swiping a hand over his chin. "Emily can be our chaperone." He laughed aloud.

Her eyes narrowed, and she shook a wet spatula at him, flinging droplets of water onto his shirt. "If you think I'm going to travel two days alone with a man who is not my husband, you have another think coming, Mr. Michaels."

"Please, please." He held up his hands and took a step back. "I was only kidding. We'll figure something out."

"Oh," she said, appearing slightly mollified. "See that you do 'figure something out' or the deal is off."

"I promise."

Silence filled the air between them as she resumed her chore.

Finally, Dell shifted and stood. "Can you make a list of the supplies you'll be needing for say, oh a month to be on the safe side, just in case there are delays?"

"All right," Cassidy said with a nod.

"That includes new shoes." His gaze slid over the black muslin. "And a new dress or two if you deem it necessary. In the meantime I'll go and talk to the wagon master—uh, what's his name?"

A small smile lifted the corners of her lips, captivating him with its soft fullness.

"Lewis Cross. He'll be at the front of the train. His wife and daughter are traveling with us."

He lifted his eyes to meet her gaze. "Can you have a list ready in an hour?"

She nodded. Clearing her throat, she lowered her eyes. "Dell, you are free, of course, to take your meals with us on the trail."

Something inside of Dell softened at the gesture. "I appreciate it," he replied truthfully. "I sure didn't relish the idea of eating my own cooking."

She glanced at him and gave a low, throaty laugh.

Dell swallowed hard. *This is going to be tougher than I thought.*

Placing his hat atop his head, he mounted his horse and rode away.

❧

Dell found the wagon master enjoying a cup of coffee at his fire. Dismounting, he lifted a large hand in greeting. "Hello, Mr. Cross."

The wagon master's weathered face remained stony. "Should I know you, Mister?"

Dell removed his hat and shook his head. "No, Sir. There's no reason for you to know me 'til now. Name's Michaels. Dell Michaels."

"What can I do for you, Mr. Michaels?"

Dell cleared his throat and pulled out the signed contract. He handed it over to Mr. Cross and waited while the man read it.

"So, Miss Sinclair will be leaving the train with you?"

"Eventually. The turnoff to the ranch is a good two weeks travel, and I'd sure appreciate it if you'd allow us to continue with the wagon train until then."

Mr. Cross hesitated. "It's been rough going for Cassidy. She must be pretty desperate to consider this without even meeting the man she's agreeing to marry. Fact is, I've been making some inquiries for a position in town. Haven't found her anything yet, though."

"I'll take full responsibility for Miss Sinclair and Emily, of course."

"She might prefer to work as a seamstress."

Dell's throat went dry. He didn't want Cassidy to stay in town. He wanted her company for as long as possible.

"The life she's being offered is a good one. But of course you can give her the choice."

"I just might."

"And if she chooses to go with me?"

The leathery wagon master nodded. "Don't suppose it'd hurt anything to have another pair of hands and an extra gun around here. Those pesky Indians are stirrin' up trouble again. Gonna have to go through Colorado this time around so my people get to Santa Fe with their scalps on their heads."

"Thank you, Sir." Dell mounted the roan. "I'll be on my way now so I can stock up on supplies and be ready to move out in the morning."

"Mr. Michaels." The wagon master squinted up at him. "I'm not crazy about this arrangement between you and Miss Sinclair. She's a fine woman and deserves more than marriage to a stranger. I'll be watching you, and if I think there's anything strange about this setup, I'll take her and the little girl all the way to Santa Fe, myself."

Dell nodded. "I'd expect no less from you."

"Welcome aboard. We leave at first light."

The two men shook hands and Dell rode away.

❧

Cassidy grimaced as the reins cut into her raw hands. Worn through from the weeks on the trail, her gloves were little or no protection against blisters so she didn't bother to wear them anymore.

Why hadn't she thought to put a new pair of gloves on the list? She knew the answer to that. Dell had already paid for so much, including a yoke of oxen to replace the ragged mules, as well as a new wagon. The less she accepted from Mr. St. John, the less she'd have to pay back in housework if she couldn't stand the man.

Or if he doesn't want me.

The thought had occurred to her more than once. After all, no one had taken the slightest romantic interest in her before. This Mr. St. John might want a dainty, doting wife rather than a woman, large and strong. Cassidy knew her face wasn't ugly, but neither was she pretty by any stretch of the imagination. Of course, how handsome could Wendell St. John III be if he had to advertise for a wife?

A flash of lightning caught Cassidy's attention from the corner of her eye. She scanned the horizon and anxiety gnawed at her as she noted thick black clouds blanketing the sky, threatening to burst at any moment.

"Emily, get back in the wagon," she called. "Looks like we're in for a storm."

"Aw, Aunt Cass." Emily obeyed but let her displeasure be known by a puckered brow.

Cassidy let out a frustrated breath. She'd have to get Emily back under control. Though she knew God expected her to train the child up with discipline, it had been difficult to punish her since her father's death.

Stopping the wagon, she waited for Emily, who flounced over and climbed up.

"I think Mr. Cross will call a halt soon, judging from the weather," Cassidy said, trying to draw Emily from her foul mood.

"Hello, Ladies."

Emily brightened considerably. "Hi, Mr. Michaels."

He touched the brim of his hat and grinned broadly at the child.

"Aunt Cass is making me sit in the wagon, and I want to walk."

Cassidy couldn't resist a wry grin at her niece's transparent attempt to gain an ally.

Dell nodded but looked at her sternly. "Couldn't help overhearing. Your Aunt Cass is right. The train's already starting to move into a circle. You'd better stay put." He turned his attention to Cassidy. "Lewis thinks we're in for a pretty bad storm, so brace yourself. I came to help you get everything tightened down. Don't want to lose anything."

"Thank you, but it isn't necessary." Cassidy maneuvered her wagon into place in the circle. "There isn't anything here I can't take care of, and there are others who will need your help more than I."

Cassidy wrapped the reins around the brake and jumped down from the wagon. She glanced up at Dell, noting a bewildered look on his face.

"Something wrong?" she questioned, a frown creasing her brow.

"What's that get-up you're wearing?"

With a glance at her attire, she smiled. "It's called a bloomer outfit."

"But you're wearing trousers!"

Thunder rumbled, and flashes of lightning were getting closer.

"Technically, they're bloomers," Cassidy replied distractedly, eyeing the sky nervously.

"They look like trousers," he insisted.

"So? I'm wearing a dress over them," she replied with a shrug.

"A short dress." Dell gaze swooped downward. "It doesn't even cover your ankles." He sounded scandalized.

"The bloomers cover my ankles." She looked down at her loose-fitting dress, which reached midway between her knee and ankles. Why was he acting so silly about it? "Don't you think there are more important things to consider right now? Lightning striking the oxen, for instance."

He ignored the remark. "Doesn't seem like a very good example for a young girl like Emily."

Miffed, Cassidy tossed her head. "You try wearing a dress with all those petticoats and see how comfortable you are out here on the trail." A loud clap of thunder punctuated her heated statement. "Seems to me, I'm teaching my niece to have some common sense, even if some menfolk would rather see a woman in a dress on a dusty trail."

"I like Aunt Cass's bloomer outfit. She said she might make one for me, if she has time."

Dell's expression softened at Emily's interruption.

"Is that so, little miss? Are you going to be an independent woman like your aunt?"

Cassidy's cheeks grew warm, but she lifted her chin. She had to be independent, didn't she? She had her niece to care for.

"I don't know," Emily replied.

The tender smile Dell sent Emily melted Cassidy's anger. He certainly would make a fine father. An unreasonable pang of jealousy hit her full in the stomach at the thought of him marrying another woman. She placed a hand over her waist as if to ward off the blow. What right did she have to be jealous? It wasn't as though a man as handsome and wonderful as Dell would ever be interested in the likes of her, anyway. And if by some miracle he were interested, it wouldn't matter because she'd signed a contract with Mr. St.

John. At the very least, she owed the rancher a chance to take one look at her and send her packing.

Cassidy shook herself from her thoughts. There was no sense in borrowing trouble. "I'd better unhitch the team before they get spooked and run away," she said, moving to do so.

Dell dismounted and placed a large hand over hers. "I'll do it for you."

Cassidy winced, catching her lip between her teeth.

"What's wrong?" he asked with a frown.

"Nothing." She tried to pull away.

He pursed his lips, turning her hand palm up. "These are badly blistered," he admonished, the concern in his voice warming her down to her toes. Intently, he gazed into her eyes. "Why didn't you wear gloves?"

Cassidy looked at the ground and swallowed hard. She shrugged. "I don't know."

"Her gloves wore out a long time ago," Emily piped up.

"Emily, get inside the wagon before the rain starts," Cassidy ordered.

The little girl's face clouded over with hurt, but, mercifully, she did as she was told.

"Look at me," Dell commanded, placing a finger beneath Cassidy's chin and lifting her head until they were face to face. "Why didn't you tell me you needed gloves?"

"I didn't think I would." She jumped as another loud clap of thunder shook the air. "That storm's getting closer, Dell. I really need to get the oxen unhitched."

"Go inside with Emily. I'll unhitch the team." He gave her a gentle nudge toward the wagon.

"B–but what about the others? They need you."

"They can take care of themselves. I'm staying right here."

A large gust of wind whipped at Cassidy's skirt and nearly knocked her off her feet as the sky opened, pouring rain on the band of travelers.

"Get inside." Dell ducked his head against the blast of wind and pushed toward the oxen.

Ignoring his order, she rushed to unhitch the other side. Soon, the oxen were free of the wagon.

"Get inside, Cassidy!" Dell yelled again, pulling at the reins. With nothing else to do, she obeyed.

꙳

Heavy rain assaulted the prairie for two days, delaying the train and dumping several inches of water on the ground. Cassidy gave up trying to build a fire after the first day, and she and Emily, with Dell as their guest, subsisted on dried meat and cold beans.

When the skies finally cleared, the people were anxious to head out. But the muddy rain-soaked ground prevented any movement. Details of women gathered drinking water. The children set about collecting buffalo chips for the fires, and the men took turns guarding the camp and hunting fresh game.

Cassidy's hands were healing, and she dreaded having them blister again once the order was given to move out.

Stepping out of the warmth and dryness of her wagon on the third day after the rain had begun, Cassidy glanced at the puddles of water on the ground and sighed. She'd be soaked before she made it back to the wagon. She dreaded stepping down from her canvas-covered home.

"Might as well get it over with," she grumbled to herself. Gathering her water buckets, she set off for the river a few yards beyond the camp, keeping her eyes firmly fixed on the ground to avoid as many puddles as possible.

"Miss Sinclair?" Mrs. Marcus, wife of the Rev. Marcus, stood before her with her own buckets filled.

"Hello," Cassidy said. "How are you faring after all this rain?"

Mrs. Marcus gave her a rosy smile. "The Lord has kept us well and as dry as can be expected, I suppose."

Cassidy inclined her head, feeling suddenly ashamed at her foul mood. "We can be thankful it wasn't any worse."

"Yes," Mrs. Marcus agreed. "As a matter of fact, that's what I wanted to discuss with you. My husband is conducting a service at our campfire tonight, and we would love for you and Emily to attend."

A thrill shot through Cassidy at the thought of having fellowship with other believers again. Thus far on the trail, they'd had few opportunities, and none since leaving Council Grove a week earlier. "We'll be there."

"Wonderful. We'll look forward to seeing you after supper."

Mrs. Marcus continued her way back to the camp, and Cassidy resumed her trek to the river. Once she reached the grassy bank, she stooped to fill her buckets. At the thought of the meeting that night, anticipation welled in her soul, and she broke into a hymn of praise.

As she straightened, her heart leaped at the sight of Dell leaning casually against a nearby tree, watching her.

"It's a good thing I wasn't an Indian sneaking up on you," he admonished lightly. "If I had been, I'd already have that pretty ginger-colored hair hanging from my belt."

"Then it's lucky for me you aren't an Indian," she retorted, feeling her cheeks grow warm at his compliment.

Dell chuckled and reached for the heavy buckets she carried. "Why are you so happy?"

"Reverend Marcus is holding a Bible meeting tonight." Cassidy couldn't keep the enthusiasm out of her voice. "Will you attend?"

"No."

Cassidy frowned at his clipped answer.

"Aren't you a believer?"

"Let's put it this way. I believe if there is a God, He isn't very interested in humanity."

Cassidy gasped, placing a hand to her chest. "Dell, don't say that."

His mouth curved into an amused smile. "Afraid of thunder and lightning from heaven?" He leaned in closer. "Don't be," he said in a conspiratorial tone. "The skies seem to be clear. As a matter of fact, Lewis gave the okay to move out tomorrow."

She stopped walking and crossed her arms in determination.

"Dell Michaels, don't you dare make light of the Lord in my presence again." Cassidy could feel her lips quiver, and tears blurred her vision. "God is the only constant in my life, and I will not stand for blasphemy."

"Cassidy," he said, the regret in his voice unmistakable. "Forgive me, please. I didn't mean to hurt you. Listen, I do believe in God. At one time we were on pretty good terms, but now. . ."

"Now?" Cassidy prodded.

"Let's just say He and I have some things to work out. I'm sorry."

A fleeting look of pain clouded his blue eyes, melting Cassidy's heart. Though there were times she didn't understand why things happened the way they did, she had never considered turning away from God for any reason. But she had known a woman back home in Missouri who had blamed God after losing her little boy to whooping cough. Cassidy's heart twisted as she wondered what had become of her.

"Do you forgive me?" Dell asked, drawing her from her memories.

Cassidy knew it certainly wasn't her place to judge Dell, but if he had gone through a heartbreak similar to that of her friend, he would find no peace until God healed him. She wanted Dell to allow God to do that. Life was difficult enough, even when one drew on a strength from above; without a relationship with God, Cassidy couldn't imagine how anyone survived the hardships.

Slowly, she lifted the buckets from his hands. "You don't need my forgiveness, Dell," she said softly. "But I truly believe whatever issues you have with God will only be settled once you surrender your heart to Him and accept His peace."

Dell remained silent, looking past her, though it appeared he stared at nothing in particular. After a moment, Cassidy realized he wasn't going to respond, so she bid him good day and stepped toward the circle of wagons, sloshing water on the ground as she left him to wrestle with her words.

three

Seated on the ground with her back against a wagon wheel for support, Cassidy watched Dell romp with the children. The pleasant aroma of strong coffee wafted from her fire, and the gentle hum of quiet singing could be heard as the women washed their supper pots and went about their nightly rituals, readying their families for bed. This was quickly becoming her favorite time of the day.

Since Dell had only a bedroll and a few personal items, his chores were minimal compared to the duties of the family men in the wagon train. In the evenings, while the other men made repairs to their wagons or cared for their teams, he played tag, blind man's bluff, baseball, or anything else the children could coax him into. Cassidy grinned. It certainly didn't take much to convince him. He was a big kid at heart and loved to play.

She leaned her head back and smiled while Emily tied a handkerchief behind Dell's head and turned him around three times. Dell was such a wonderful man. If only he would come to the Bible meetings, Cassidy knew God would be able to get through to him. He'd said nothing about their encounter during the rain delay, and Cassidy hadn't mentioned it either. But she had prayed for him often. Somehow, she felt she should do everything possible to encourage Dell to reconcile his relationship with the Lord.

The campers had enjoyed the worship service during the three-day rain delay so much, that once they returned to the trail, they gathered around the preacher's fire a couple of evenings a week and worshiped together. But Dell never joined them.

"I got someone!" he yelled, yanking the blindfold from his

face and tickling the towheaded boy held captive in his arms.

A giggle escaped Cassidy's lips, and Dell raised his head. His eyes still twinkled from the game as his gaze met hers. Her pulse quickened, and she quickly shifted her attention to Emily.

"Time to get ready for bed," she called, waiting for Emily to protest. She wasn't disappointed.

"Aw, Aunt Cass. It's hardly even dark, yet."

"Now, Sweetheart," Dell admonished the little girl. "You do as your aunt says, or she might not let us play together anymore."

A look of uncertainty clouded Emily's pea green eyes, and she wrinkled her freckled nose. "Okay." She flounced to the wagon. Bending over, she gave Cassidy a kiss and a hug. " 'Night."

Dell removed his hat and extended a hand to Cassidy. "Like some help up from there?"

Warily, she accepted his assistance but clutched the wheel for support.

Shaking his head, he chuckled, throwing Emily a sideways glance. "A guy drops your aunt one time—just once—and she doubts his manly strength from then on."

"Honestly." Cassidy rolled her eyes but felt her face growing hot.

Her gaze riveted to Dell's head as he ran long fingers through the mass of dark hair molded into the shape of his hat and curling up at the ends. He needed a haircut pretty badly.

"I suppose I ought to find someone who'll cut it for me," he said self-consciously, as though reading her thoughts. "I don't suppose you would. . ."

Horrified, Cassidy opened her mouth to refuse, but Emily interrupted her.

"Aunt Cass always used to cut my pa's hair."

"Emily!"

"Well, you did. Why can't you—"

"Run along now. I'll be in to pray with you shortly."

"Yes, Ma'am," she said with a heavy sigh.

"Good night, Emily," Dell called with a wink, flashing the little girl a smile.

She grinned broadly back at him. " 'Night," she replied, crawling into the wagon.

Slowly, Cassidy met his gaze. His eyes pleaded in child-like innocence, amusement written plainly on his handsome face. He was enjoying this a little too much!

A sudden idea formed in her mind, and she couldn't resist a slight smile. Perhaps this opportunity was providential. "Let's make a deal." She stood, her feet shoulder-width apart. She folded her arms across her chest and tilted her head to one side.

Dell lifted an eyebrow. "Like a wager?"

"Certainly not a wager. I don't gamble."

"Of course you don't gamble. I didn't mean to imply anything improper." He drew a short breath. "A bargain then."

She nodded. "Yes."

Following her example, he folded his arms over his chest as well. "Let's hear what you have to say."

"I'll give you a much-needed haircut. . ." Her voice rang with challenge. "If you attend the service with Emily and me tomorrow night."

His eyes narrowed. "Hmm. . . You drive a hard bargain for a woman." A short nod accompanied his next words. "You have a deal, Cassidy Sinclair."

Stunned, she accepted the proffered hand. "I do? Are you sure?"

A wry grin played at Dell's lips. "I guess it's worth it," he drawled. "You're not backing out, are you?"

"Of course not. I'll cut it right after breakfast, then. If you're really sure."

His eyes twinkled at her discomfiture. "I'm sure." His voice was smooth like honey as he gripped her hand, sealing the bargain.

A tremor shot through Cassidy at the warmth of his touch, and she pulled away quickly. "Good night, Dell."

He flashed her a heart-stopping grin and placed his Stetson hat atop his head. "I'll see you in the morning."

Cassidy couldn't drag her eyes from him as he strode into the night, whistling to himself. Once he was out of sight she clapped a frustrated hand to her forehead. The thought of being close enough to Dell to cut his hair sent shivers down her spine, and warmth crept through her belly. He had made it clear he wasn't interested in the services, so it never occurred to her he'd really accept. She'd only offered because she wanted another excuse to invite him to the meeting in a way that wouldn't seem preachy.

With an angry toss of her head, she doused the campfire. How dare she have these thoughts and feelings about Dell when she'd signed a contract with Mr. St. John! Of course, she didn't have to marry the rancher. She could simply keep house for him. Then she would be free to marry Dell. Marry Dell! What was she thinking? Dreaming like a schoolgirl— that's what she was doing. It was just that every time he looked at her, he made her feel. . .beautiful.

Well, you aren't beautiful, Cassidy Sinclair, she chided herself. *And you better just forget about romantic notions and stick to the bargain.*

Besides, Dell wasn't interested in God right now. She couldn't have these feelings for him. It just wasn't right, was it?

❧

Dell noticed a hesitation in Cassidy's eyes when he approached the camp. He felt a guilty sense of glee at her discomfiture. When she had given him the challenge, he knew she expected him to refuse. But something inside of him had recognized a good excuse to join the worshipers, and the refusal on his lips had turned to acceptance, surprising him almost as much as it had her.

Emily looked up dully from where she sat on the tongue of the wagon. Instead of greeting him with her usual exuberance, she leaned forward and tucked her chin in her hand. "Morning, Mr. Michaels."

Dell smiled. He'd never seen the little girl so subdued. Hoping to cheer her, he reached out and ruffled her hair. "Hey, Kiddo. You in trouble again?"

She shook her head.

Dell frowned.

"What's wrong, Honey?" he asked, placing a hand on her forehead. He glanced at Cassidy. "She feels feverish."

Cassidy wiped her hands on a towel and walked the short distance to her niece. Cupping Emily's chin, she looked into the little girl's flushed face. "She certainly does," she said, a worried frown creasing her brow.

"Aunt Cass, I don't feel good."

"Sweetie, do you feel like having breakfast?"

Emily shook her head miserably. "May I lie down?"

"Of course. Come along, and I'll get you all tucked in." Cassidy helped a shaky Emily to her feet and walked around to the back of the wagon. "I'll be with you in a little while," she told Dell over her shoulder.

When she returned twenty minutes later, the worried frown was still in place. "I wish there was a doctor among us."

"Sit," Dell ordered, handing her a tin cup filled with coffee. "What seems to be the ailment?"

"She complains of a headache and sore throat. Plus—"

"The fever," Dell finished.

Cassidy nodded, her shoulders sagging. His heart went out to her. She had already lost her brother. It was inconceivable that she should lose Emily, too.

"Two children have died from sickness since we set out just a few weeks ago. Oh, Dell, I can't bear the thought of losing Emily. She's all the family I have left in the world." Large tears rolled down her cheeks.

He closed the short distance between them in two long strides. Enfolding her in his arms, he stroked her hair. "Emily will be fine, Cass. I'm sure by tomorrow she'll be back to running around making trouble again."

Cassidy pulled away and gazed hopefully into his eyes. "Oh, I hope you're right. Sickness just comes on so sudden out here and there's nothing anyone can do about it. W—what if it's cholera?"

"Do you want me to get Reverend Marcus to come and pray with you?"

Surprise lit her jade green eyes. "Why, yes. If you wouldn't mind."

"I'll be right back, then," he replied.

A moment later, Dell interrupted the preacher's breakfast with the news of Emily's illness.

Without hesitation, Reverend Marcus grabbed his Bible and kissed his wife good-bye. "I'll be back when I'm no longer needed."

Mrs. Marcus reached up and patted her husband's face. "Take your time, and come back when the Lord releases you. And tell Cassidy if she needs anything to let me know."

Admiration flickered inside Dell, and an odd sense of longing filled his heart.

Reverend Marcus clamped his black hat atop his head. "Let's go."

While the men strode toward Cassidy's wagon, the preacher began to pray. "Father, I ask for Your healing touch for little Emily. And while You work the cure, please give Miss Sinclair peace."

Stirred by the simple prayer, Dell surprised himself by muttering an "amen."

Cassidy was pacing before the wagon as they reached her. Relief lit her face when she spied the reverend. She quickly ushered him into the wagon while Dell watched from outside.

Emily stirred as they prayed, and her glassy eyes fluttered open. "Reverend," she whispered.

"Hello, Emily," the kind man replied, taking a freckled hand in his.

"Preach really good tonight, 'cause Dell's coming to the meeting."

"He is?"

Emily nodded, wearily. "Aunt Cass is going to cut his hair. . . ."

The preacher's eyes twinkled as he threw Dell a grin. "Well, that is an answer to prayer."

"Uh-huh," Emily said, eyes fluttering shut.

"I'm going to go now, Sweetie. But God is taking care of you. Do you believe that?"

Again, Emily nodded, a small trembly smile touching her lips. She fell asleep before the preacher climbed down out of the wagon.

Dell shifted his feet as the minister glanced his way.

"We'll expect to see you this evening," he said.

"I suppose so." Dell swallowed hard.

"I'll reserve a seat for you right close then, so you're sure to hear every word."

"Sure, Reverend. You do that."

"Well, I better go prepare something especially good for tonight, per Emily's request."

Just then Cassidy stepped up to them. "Good-bye," she said, shaking the preacher's hand, "and thanks for coming."

"Anytime." He focused his attention back on Dell. "I'll see you later." Stuffing his hands into his pockets, he strolled away, whistling a hymn.

Dell glanced at Cassidy's face, studying the exquisite curve of her chin and the softness of her full lips. Large, luminous eyes gave her an air of vulnerability, and he couldn't help thinking how the delicateness of her face contrasted with her sturdy build. Even though he stood taller than most men, Cassidy almost met him eye to eye. She wasn't fat, but neither was she scrawny. Her small waist accented her curved hips. One thing was for certain—he couldn't get her out of his mind. He hadn't thought about a woman this way for a long time.

Her head shifted slightly until her eyes met his gaze.

Clearing her throat, she motioned for him to sit. "I'll get you some breakfast."

"You sit, Cass." He took the spoon from her hand. "Let me serve you today."

He dipped the cinnamon-laced oatmeal into two bowls and handed one to her.

"Thank you."

They ate in relative and unaccustomed silence.

Finally, Dell cleared his throat. "Why don't you go sit with Emily? If she gets to feeling better you can cut my hair later."

"Yes, I think I will," she replied. Throwing him a grateful smile, she set down her half-empty bowl, and climbed back into the wagon.

Dell wiped the dishes and left the camp. He smiled as a thought came to him.

There was no question about it. He was smitten with Cassidy Sinclair.

❧

Cassidy woke to a light tapping outside of the wagon. She reached over and placed a gentle hand on Emily's forehead. Drenched in sweat, the little girl was cool to the touch.

"Thank You, Lord," Cassidy whispered and crawled to the flap.

Dell stood staring up at her. Those eyes—bluer than the cloudless sky—squinted in the bright sun.

"How is she?"

"Still asleep, but her fever's broken."

Noting the relief on his face, she smiled. "You're fond of Emily, aren't you?"

"Secret's out, eh?" He grinned, reaching to help her down.

Without thought, she slid effortlessly into his arms. Heat rose to her cheeks when he didn't let go. She felt his muscles twitch as her hands pressed flat against his chest. Raising her eyes to meet his, Cassidy caught her breath at the intensity of his gaze.

"You know what?" His voice was low and husky, sending shivers through her.

"Wh–what?"

"I think we're finally getting this right."

"This?"

"No more tumbling to the ground. 'Course that wasn't so bad, either."

"Dell!"

"I can't help it," he said, his face coming closer to hers. "With you in my arms, all rational thought escapes me."

His breath was warm on her face, and her eyes shifted to his mouth. It curved into a smile, then formed her name. "Cassidy," he whispered.

Swallowing hard, she closed her eyes and waited.

"Hello, Miss Sinclair. Mr. Michaels." A singsong voice broke through the mist and Cassidy's eyes flew open. She stared, horrified, as the Pike sisters strolled by, curiosity plainly written on their pinched faces.

"Miss Pike." With Cassidy still in his arms, Dell nodded first to one and then the other. "Miss Pike. Beautiful day, isn't it?" He flashed a wide smile, showing perfect white teeth.

The two spinsters blushed to the roots of their hair. "We. . . uh. . .heard little Emily was sick and wondered if there was something we could do."

Cassidy squirmed in Dell's grasp, but his arms tightened about her. "That's very thoughtful of you both," she replied. "But she appears to be over the worst of it."

With a quick glance at Dell's arms wrapped around Cassidy, the two women gave a simultaneous nod and walked quickly past, whispering to each other.

"Thought they'd never leave," he murmured. "Now where were we?" His gaze roved dangerously over her face, resting on her lips.

"Oh, no you don't, Mister." Cassidy pushed her way out of his arms. "Don't you dare kiss me in public view."

"So you wouldn't mind in private?"

With a gasp at his play on words, Cassidy looked him squarely in the eye. "This isn't a proper topic of conversation," she said firmly. "I have a contract with Mr. St. John and I intend to hold to my end of the bargain. Shame on you for being so disloyal to the man who sent you to find him a wife!"

"You were about to let me kiss you," he reminded her, with a slow drawl.

"I most certainly was not going to let you kiss me."

Dell looked stunned, but amused. "Do I still get my haircut?"

With only a moment's hesitation, Cassidy nodded. "Sit. I'll get my shears."

She climbed into the wagon and opened her sewing kit, retrieving her scissors. "Oh, Lord. Keep me strong." She cast a glance at the sleeping child and started to climb down.

"Need some help?" Dell called, his voice thick with amusement.

"I think not." Gathering her skirts about her, she carefully climbed backward out of the wagon.

"Are you still mad?" Dell asked when she returned.

"Yes. How could you embarrass me in front of the wagon train's source of information? By nightfall the entire camp will know about this."

"Hmm," Dell said. "You are mad. Am I safe while you stand over me with a sharp object?"

"I assure you, you're safe—from bodily injury anyway." She smiled mischievously. "Of course there are no guarantees I won't accidentally cut your hair crooked."

Dell gave her a worried frown. "Hey, now. You wouldn't mess up my hair just because I found myself irresistibly drawn to your beauty and tried to steal a kiss, would you?"

How could he tease her about her looks?

"Beauty, huh?" she quipped. "Let's not make this into a fairy tale."

He frowned, but she gave him no chance to speak. "As to whether or not you get a decent haircut. . .that depends on how well you behave yourself."

"I'll be the perfect gentleman." He placed his left hand over his heart and raised his right hand. "So help me God."

"Hmmph. Considering your relationship with God—or

rather your lack of one—that doesn't exactly reassure me," she retorted. "Now let's get this over with. You have a promise to keep to my niece."

❧

The worshipers sat on the ground around the glowing campfire, listening to the Reverend Marcus's full, rich voice sharing enthusiastically from his worn, black Bible.

Filled with nervous energy, Dell shifted uncomfortably and resisted the urge to bolt from the service. He hadn't attended a church service since Anna died, and even in this open setting, he felt out of place.

He barely heard a word Reverend Marcus spoke as his mind stayed riveted to memories of the day he walked away from God. The God who took Anna and left him with four children to raise alone. It wasn't right. Anna was the gentlest and kindest creature he'd ever known, and the world was a cruel place without her. God should have known how much he needed her. And what of the children? The youngest, four-year-old Jack, had never known his mother. Dell had begged God to spare her life, but He hadn't. She hemorrhaged and was gone without ever laying eyes on their fourth child.

"Dell?" The preacher's gentle voice broke through his hypnotic state, and Dell lifted his head, noting through his daze that everyone was gone but him.

Tears streamed down his face.

"It wasn't God's fault. He kept His end of the bargain. It was mine. I couldn't control myself—couldn't keep my hands off her. She kept having babies until finally. . ." He took in great gulps of air as sobs racked his body. "When our third child was born, she was having such a difficult time of it, and we were afraid we would lose her. I promised if God would just let her live, I'd never touch her again. And then I. . .I killed her." A groan came from somewhere deep inside him. He jammed his fist into his gut to ease the ache. "Why didn't I keep my end of the deal?"

Reverend Marcus placed a hand on Dell's shoulder. "God

doesn't bargain with man, Son. His ways are too high for that."

"But He pulled her through when I made a deal with Him and took her when I broke my side of the agreement."

The older man lowered himself to the ground next to Dell. "The rain falls on the righteous and the unrighteous, Son. There are no guarantees in this life."

Dell frowned. Here he was pouring his heart out to this man, and he was quoting vague Scripture verses? Was that supposed to comfort him? Bitterly, he wiped his eyes and stood. He should have known better. There was no peace to be had at a Bible meeting. "Thanks for your time, Reverend."

"Wait. Do you understand what I just quoted to you?"

" 'Fraid not." Dell's lips twisted into a bitter smile.

"It means no one is exempt from life. Your wife could have just as easily died from an Indian attack or a fire."

"But she didn't," Dell insisted. "She died because I didn't stay away from her."

"Did you force yourself on her?"

Dell tensed, resentment creeping through him at the very suggestion. "Of course not. I loved my wife. Things were good between us—that way."

"Then your wife knew the risk of having another child. Correct?"

Dell nodded.

Reverend Marcus placed a firm hand on Dell's shoulder. "She made her choice, and life dealt a harsh blow. Don't blame God. Accept His comfort and move forward."

With a need to be alone, Dell smiled slightly. "I'd best be bedding down for the night, Rev."

"May I give you a bit of advice?"

"Sure."

"I don't know what your relationship is to Miss Sinclair and Emily, but I've seen you together. I strongly urge you to get your heart right with God before settling on a permanent relationship with those two."

"I'll think about it. Thanks." Dell raised a hand in farewell, intending to take a walk down by the river. But as though they had a mind of their own, his feet led him toward Cassidy's campsite.

He spied her leaning against the wagon, the gentle breeze blowing wisps of loose hair around her face and throat as she stared into the night sky. His throat constricted, and he drew a deep, unsteady breath. If everything went well, they'd be leaving the wagon train in a few days. It was time to tell her the truth. He only hoped she didn't run away. Though it might be better for them both if she did.

four

Cassidy stood silently watching Dell approach. Her pulse quickened at the determination on his face. Something was wrong.

"How's Emily?" he asked, concern edging his voice.

"Sleeping. Her fever never returned, thank God. How was the service?"

Dell shrugged. "I've been to worse, I suppose."

Hiding her disappointment, she moved to the fire and poured him a cup of coffee. Settling onto the ground against the wagon wheel, she patted the earth beside her.

"Sit. Tell me what's wrong."

"What do you mean?"

"You're as skittish as a wild stallion. I expect you to bolt any second."

With a heavy sigh, he dropped down beside her and took a sip of the coffee.

"I have something to tell you," he said slowly, avoiding her gaze.

A sense of dread filled Cassidy at his solemn tone of voice.

He cleared his throat nervously then began to speak. "I should have told you before now, but I was afraid you'd. . ." Raking fingers through his freshly cut hair, he emitted a groan. "Oh, Cassidy, I'm just going to come right out and say it. I'm Wendell St. John. It was my ad posted at the general store."

A knot formed in Cassidy's stomach. "Why?"

"We didn't exactly get off to a good start," he said with a wry, humorless smile. "Remember my 'insufferable manners'?"

She shot to her feet, anger coursing through her veins, and

45

turned to face him. "I'm beginning to," she replied, fearing her trembling legs might not hold her.

"I saw the look on your face when you thought I had posted the ad. You were so mortified, I was afraid you might not agree to come if you knew it was me."

"I see." She folded her arms over her chest. "So you lied."

He nodded. "I'm sorry."

"So why tell me now?" she challenged. "What makes you think I won't change my mind while I can still travel on with the wagon train?"

He reached into his shirt pocket and pulled out a folded document. "Are you forgetting this?"

Cassidy snatched the contract from Dell's hand. She read it carefully by the flickering firelight. Sure enough, there were no clauses for lying, sneaky ranchers. "What are you going to do? Have me hung for breaking this?"

He pulled his legs up, resting his forearms on his knees. With his coffee cup clasped between both hands, he sighed. "Of course not." His gaze caught and held hers. "But I hope you'll consider coming to the ranch with me. My children have been without a mother long enough. They need you."

Cassidy thought back to the notice. It had read, "Must love children." She narrowed her eyes. "How many children do you have?" Her voice was low but firm.

"Four."

It was her turn to sigh. "With Emily that would be. . ."

"Five. I know. I've already counted." His face held a look of hope. "Will you consider marrying me?"

Cassidy ducked her head. Her first marriage proposal. It wasn't exactly as she'd dreamed. No bending on one knee with words of undying love and devotion. Still, who was she to quibble about technique? She wasn't likely to get another offer of marriage anytime soon. After all, it had taken thirty-five years to get this one.

Her heart did a little dance. He wanted to marry her. Dell. Wonderful, funny, handsome Dell. She frowned. No. Not her

Dell. Wendell. Lying, cheating, sneaky, say-anything-to-get-my-way Wendell.

"Cassidy?"

She glanced up, fury rising within her all over again. "You took advantage of the precarious position I was in. How do I know I can ever trust you?" She stamped her foot and stepped closer, wagging a finger in his direction. "Maybe you don't even have a ranch or children."

Dell shot to his feet. "I'll be back," he said firmly. "Don't go anywhere."

Cassidy paced along the length of the wagon. *I should just go inside the wagon right now and ignore him when he knocks. Of course, being the kind of man he is, he'd probably just come right in.*

Her cheeks burned at this last thought. "Lord, please tell me what's right," she beseeched.

Before the answer could arrive, Dell was back, shoving a daguerreotype into her hands.

"What's this?

"The proper question is, who are these lovely children?" he replied with a smile.

"Then what's the proper answer?"

"They're mine."

Cassidy glanced down at the images of four lovely children.

"This is Tarah." He indicated a young lady with soft eyes. Her regal bone structure gave her the appearance of a queen granting favors to her subjects by allowing the image to be taken. "She's sixteen."

"She's beautiful."

"Yes," he drawled, a smirk touching his lips. "She knows it, too."

There was pride in his voice, and Cassidy's heart warmed.

"Then there's Sam, next in line. He's fourteen."

"Very handsome."

Dell lifted his eyebrow and flashed her a grin. "Everyone says he looks like me."

Cassidy rolled her eyes. "Who's this?" she asked, pointing to a cherubic, round-faced boy with blond curls covering his head.

"That's Jack. He looks like his mother."

"How old is he?"

"Four. His mother died when he was born." Dell touched a finger to the last child in the photo, a gangly boy with freckles spread across his nose. A wide mouth curved into what Cassidy could only describe as an ornery grin.

"And this is Luke. He's nine—the prankster in the family." His eyes sparkled with good-natured warning. "You'll have to watch yourself around him."

Glancing at the faces of Dell's children, an ache filled Cassidy's heart. Here was her chance to be a mother to four children who needed her. It could only be that God was filling her too-long-empty arms. First with Emily, and now these four precious souls. Her eyes roved over the face of the youngest boy again. He had never known maternal love. Surely God must want her to agree to the marriage. But how could she marry a man whose heart wasn't completely surrendered to God? Immediately, she rejected the troublesome thought. Dell had known God, so he wasn't exactly an unbeliever. He was more of a wounded soul in need of love and comfort to draw him back into the fold. When she raised her head to meet Dell's gaze, only the smallest of doubts remained in her mind. Impatiently, she pushed them aside as she became lost in a deep sea of blue eyes. "All right. I'll marry you."

The expression of shock on Dell's face was soon replaced with relief, then joy. He stepped toward her, opening his arms.

Cassidy stepped back.

His jaw tightened and the muscle by his left eye twitched as he dropped his arms. "I see. You'll be a mother, but not a wife?"

Cassidy opened her mouth to deny his words, but he continued.

"It's probably just as well. Thank you for agreeing to this. . . awkward situation." He held out his hand, and Cassidy placed her hand inside his to seal the agreement. "I promise I'll be a good pa to Emily, too. I guess we'll just have to make the best of things."

Unable to speak through the lump in her throat, Cassidy simply nodded. *Please leave now.* She hadn't meant she wouldn't be a wife to him. She just didn't want to be kissed in public. After all, it would have been her first kiss.

He had said it was just as well she didn't want to be a wife to him. The reason? He obviously didn't want her for a real wife. He simply needed a mother for his children. Tears pricked her eyes. She fought hard for composure.

As if sensing her desire to be rid of him, Dell withdrew his hand. "First thing in the morning I'll speak to Reverend Marcus about performing the ceremony."

"S so soon?"

"You're the one who refuses to travel alone with a man who isn't your husband," he drawled.

"Well." Cassidy drew herself up, primly. "It isn't proper."

"We'll be splitting off from the wagon party in three days at the most. Would you like for the ceremony to take place the evening before we leave?"

"That'll be fine. Thank you for your consideration."

"Aunt Cass, I'm thirsty," Emily called from the wagon. Cassidy prayed a silent word of thanks at the interruption.

"I'm coming, Em," she called, then turned to Dell. "I'd better. . ."

Reaching forward, Dell placed the palm of his hand against her cheek. With his forefinger, he traced a feather-light line from cheekbone to chin and spoke so softly that Cassidy could barely hear his words. "Good night, darling Cassidy. And thank you." Then he turned and left her.

She shivered and felt her lungs protest until she finally thought to breathe. Had he really called her 'darling'?"

"Aunt Cass," Emily's insistent voice called.

"Yes, Honey. I'm coming."

❧

Dell stretched out on his bedroll beneath a canopy of twinkling stars. It was a beautiful night, complete with a glorious full moon. From somewhere in the camp, he heard the lazy sound of a harmonica playing, "I'll Take You Home Again, Kathleen." The mellow music, combined with a night made for romance, brought tears of longing to his eyes.

Clearly, Cassidy wanted a marriage in name only, and he understood her need to provide a home for Emily. He supposed he could live with that arrangement. It would probably be easier. Perhaps neither he nor Cassidy was ready for a romantic relationship.

Though his mind made a convincing argument, his heart couldn't quite believe it. He'd seen longing in Cassidy's eyes when he held her in his arms earlier that day. The same longing, he knew, had been mirrored in his own. If the Pike sisters hadn't interrupted, he would have kissed Cassidy, and she would have allowed it. But that was before she had learned the truth. Oh, how he regretted not being honest with her sooner. Still, Cassidy was a sensible woman. Maybe after she had time to calm down she'd forgive him, and they could pick up where they left off.

His troubled thoughts began to shift, and Anna's image drifted to his mind. What if Cassidy did change her mind and they became man and wife in truth? Would he lose her as well? He knew he couldn't live again through the pain he'd felt at the loss of Anna.

With a groan, he flopped over on his stomach and settled his chin into his fist, as his heart flip-flopped between his desire for Cassidy and the fear of causing another woman he loved to die.

What a mess he had made of everything. He had advertised for a wife with the provision she could be a housekeeper if either decided marriage between them wouldn't work. In truth, that's what he'd intended all along. But he'd never counted on falling in love. And if he gave into his feelings once they were married, he'd risk losing Cassidy the way he'd lost Anna.

Emitting a weary sigh, he closed his eyes and drifted into a troubled sleep.

ᵃᵃ

Mrs. Marcus gently placed a bouquet of wild flowers into Cassidy's trembling hands. The vows were supposed to have been said privately before Reverend Marcus, but somehow the Pike sisters had gotten wind of the marriage, and the service had turned into a celebration for the entire wagon train.

At first Lewis Cross had refused to halt the train for the entire day, stating firmly that they must keep going. They had already lost time with the detour to Council Grove and the three-day rain delay.

Although disappointed—particularly the women—they resigned themselves to a smaller, less festive affair.

But by the next day, everyone stood in happy surprise while Lewis announced he had changed his mind. They would remain in camp for the entire day, he'd said, and everyone should go ahead with their preparations. He even called a halt at midday the day before the wedding, so the men could hunt for the celebration feast.

No one knew for sure why he'd changed his mind, but it was whispered about that Mrs. Cross had expressed her desire for a break in the rigorous routine. So Lewis gave in, but grumbled that he wouldn't be held responsible for any Indian attacks. They were in Indian country, after all, and it was better to keep moving. There was a good possibility, he'd insisted, that all their hair would be dangling from a spear before the night was over. But if they wanted to stop for a wedding—well, that was their choice.

The mention of Indians caused some unrest among the travelers. Still, a wedding didn't happen every day, and everyone looked forward to a break in their rigorous routine. So with excitement, the women of the train had pitched in and helped

Cassidy finish the new dress she'd been working on.

She'd bought the white cotton material in Council Grove with part of the money Dell had specified she use for her trousseau.

The collar trailed up the back of her neck, but dipped down in front forming a V a few inches below her throat. The bodice clung to her body and the skirt widened as far as the petticoats forced it to. Cassidy had opted for short, puffy sleeves before she knew this was to be her wedding dress, but decided to keep them short, anyway. After all, she needed a summer gown to wear to church.

The other women made pies from the wonderful gooseberries found growing wild along the trail. Two deer had been killed, as well as several squirrels. Everyone was looking forward to a tremendous feast following the nuptials.

So there she stood, trembling from head to toe, wondering why she'd ever agreed to this crazy marriage. The laughing, teasing Dell she had grown so fond of had been replaced by a sullen, moody Wendell. Anxiety gnawed at Cassidy's stomach, and she considered backing out of the marriage. But she had given her word and truly believed God had provided this avenue for Emily and herself. He would make a way for their happiness. She was sure of it. Still, although she prayed, the unrest persisted. Finally, she attributed the feeling to pre-marriage jitters and pushed it aside.

"You're a beautiful bride," she was told over and over. "Simply lovely."

With no mirror to confirm or deny the comments, she listened dubiously to the assurances of the other women.

She had washed her hair in the creek that morning, and when it dried, she left it flowing in waves down her back at Mrs. Marcus's urging. She found out why the woman had been so insistent about the issue when Emily burst into the wagon, holding a wreath of white wild flowers. "Here Aunt Cass," she said proudly. "I made this for you to wear on your head."

Tears pooled in Cassidy's eyes. "Thank you, Sweetheart. It's beautiful," she whispered. "Will you put it on for me?"

Emily nodded. Cassidy bent and allowed the child to place the wreath carefully on her head. "Oh, Aunt Cass," Emily breathed, her eyes glowing. "You're just about the prettiest thing I've ever seen."

Cassidy smiled and decided to let the exaggeration go. Today she had the right to listen to people tell her she was lovely. After all, she was finally a bride.

❧

Dell stood beside Reverend Marcus in the small grove of trees next to the river. The crowd of pioneers gathered in their finest clothes, smiling and light-hearted, ready to wish the happy couple congratulations. . .assuming the bride ever showed up.

Dell cleared his throat and drew an irritated breath. He knew she was only marrying him to mother his children, but couldn't she show a little enthusiasm for the sake of appearances? These folks didn't understand the arrangement.

For the past two days, he'd waffled between excitement over the marriage and dread over the arrangement. Cassidy had been so busy with preparations for the wedding he'd barely seen or spoken to her. The women tittered around him, inviting him to share meals with their families, obviously an attempt to keep him occupied while Cassidy worked. And worst of all, were the sly grins from the married men in the wagon train. Especially since he knew, in all likelihood, he'd be spending his wedding night on the hard wood bed of Cassidy's wagon.

That was if she hadn't changed her mind.

"Don't worry, Son." The preacher's gentle gray eyes twinkled in merriment. "She'll be here any second."

"I wouldn't count on—" He stopped mid-sentence as the crowd parted, and a murmur rose among them. Dell inhaled sharply.

Cassidy appeared like something from a dream. Standing with the sun behind her, she looked surreal. He'd never seen her hair down and flowing free like that, and he felt the urge to sink his fingers into the shimmering tresses. She walked slowly toward him. The wreath atop her head could have been a halo. As though pulled by an unseen force, she lifted her face and cast a luminous gaze upon him, taking his breath away. In spite of himself, he offered up a silent prayer of thanks. He didn't deserve this woman, didn't deserve a second chance, but somehow she was about to become his, for better or worse.

Suddenly, Dell's collar was choking him, and his palms became clammy. His knees nearly buckled as he mechanically repeated his vows and listened to Cassidy's quiet, solemn voice respond to the preacher.

"I now pronounce you man and wife. You may kiss your bride."

Dell fought to stay on his feet as his breath came in short bursts, and his head started to spin. Before he could turn to his new wife and seal the vows with a kiss, Dell felt himself sway. Then everything went black.

five

A stunned silence filled the air as Dell landed with a thud on the hard ground.

"Aunt Cass," Emily shrieked in panic. "Is he dead?"

A low rumble of laughter began in the crowd and grew to a roar as Dell opened his somewhat dazed eyes and sat up, rubbing the back of his head.

"No, Sweetie, he isn't dead."

Cassidy extended a steadying hand to her new husband, whose face glowed bright red. "Are you all right?" she asked, speaking softly enough so that only he could hear.

"Everything but my pride," he drawled, accepting her assistance as he stumbled to his feet.

Dell glanced at Reverend Marcus, who wiped tears of mirth from his round face.

"May we continue with the ceremony?" Dell asked.

The preacher gave him a bewildered look. "But the wedding is over. I pronounced you man and wife before your. . . um. . .fall."

The crowd roared again, and Cassidy wished the ground would open up and swallow her. He didn't even remember that they were already married!

"No, Sir," Dell argued. "I distinctly recall one more thing you said before I passed out cold." He grinned.

Understanding dawned upon Reverend Marcus's face. "Ah, yes," he said with a merry lilt to his voice. "You may now kiss your bride."

Before she knew what was happening, Dell grabbed Cassidy by her shoulders and turned her to face him. Slipping his hands around her waist, he drew her close. Cassidy's heart thumped wildly as she prepared for her first kiss. His head descended slowly. So achingly slow that she wrapped her arms about his neck and raised on her toes, tipping her face toward his to close the gap between them more quickly. His eyes registered surprise, then he smiled. At the touch of his lips on hers, Cassidy relaxed against him, the spectators fading into the background. There was only the feel of Dell's soft lips and of his arms holding her close.

All too soon, the moment was over, and the look in Dell's eyes left her as breathless as the kiss itself. But there was no time to analyze his gaze or her feelings, for they were surrounded by well-wishers.

As the crowd of men swept Dell away, Mrs. Marcus slipped an arm through Cassidy's and led her from the rest of the group.

"I've arranged for Emily to sleep in our wagon tonight," she whispered.

Cassidy drew back. "Whatever for?"

A twinkle lit the faded blue eyes of the plump woman standing before her. "Do you want a child in your wagon on your first night as a married woman?"

Mortified, Cassidy lifted her hand and covered her mouth. "Oh my! I never even considered. . ."

"It's all settled, then. Emily will stay with us tonight." Mrs. Marcus gave her a gentle pat on the arm.

She could only nod in response as the preacher's wife moved away to join the women preparing the celebration dinner.

Panic welled up inside Cassidy, and she looked around for a means of escape.

Her eyes scanned the camp, stopping short as her gaze locked with Dell's. He shot her a concerned frown. She ducked her head to avoid his eyes and walked hurriedly to the wagon. Climbing in, she sat down, knees to her chest, tears of humiliation streaming down her cheeks.

The flap raised and Dell stuck his head inside, worry written plainly on his handsome face. His frown deepened at her tears, and without a word, he climbed in and gathered her in his arms while she sobbed. When her tears subsided, he pulled away, holding her at arm's length. "What's wrong?"

"M–mrs. Marcus is keeping Emily in her wagon tonight so you and I can be alone." A fresh onslaught of tears rolled down her face. "Honestly, Dell, it's all so humiliating."

"Oh." He cleared his throat and appeared to be in thought for a moment. "Cassidy, look at me."

She did so, reluctantly. His gaze roamed over her face and came to rest on her mouth. Cassidy held her breath, hoping he'd kiss her once again. Instead, he lifted his hand and cupped her face, wiping away a tear from her cheek with the brush of his thumb.

"If I don't stay here tonight," he said, softly, "we'll both be laughingstocks."

"You already are," Cassidy reminded him, then clapped her hand over her mouth. "Oh, Dell, I'm sorry. How rude of me!"

His lips twisted into a wry grin. "It's true. I can't believe I passed out like that. These folks will never forget the wedding where the groom fainted."

A nervous giggle escaped her lips. Soon they were both laughing so hard tears rolled from their eyes, and Cassidy could feel some of the tension slipping away. Suddenly, Dell stopped laughing and drew her close, his face inches from hers. "You've made me very happy," he whispered. "Have you forgiven me for not telling you the truth from the beginning?"

Reaching up, Cassidy pressed a hand to his cheek. She wanted to reassure him, but she became alarmed as she realized how warm his skin felt. Pulling back, she frowned and moved her hand to his forehead, then to his other cheek. "Dell, you feel feverish. Are you sick?"

His gaze darted away from her. "I think it's just all the excitement. I've never fainted before."

Cassidy was about to pursue the subject further, when they heard voices outside the wagon.

"Hey, you two, get out here and join the celebration. You can't leave your wedding guests to fend for themselves."

Cassidy's cheeks burned. How much more humiliation must she endure on a day that should have been the happiest of her whole life?

"Oh, Dell," she groaned.

"They're only teasing. Besides, I have a right to be in here. I'm your husband."

That didn't exactly make her feel any better, especially now that she wasn't sure what to expect from him.

"Let's go join them, shall we, Mrs. St. John?"

The name sounded strange, foreign, but somehow. . .right. "I suppose we should," she agreed with a sigh. "I–if you're sure you feel up to it."

"I wouldn't miss our wedding celebration for anything in the world. Don't worry." Dell hopped down from the wagon and reached up for her.

Cassidy accepted his help, but seeing the gleam in his eyes, she stepped quickly from his arms. "Behave yourself," she admonished.

The newlyweds received a round of applause as, hand in hand, they moved into the center of the circled wagons and sat at their "table" fashioned from boards placed atop packing crates.

The feast was "scrumptious," according to Emily. But to Cassidy, whose nerves were taut, it tasted like cooked burlap. Dell sat by her side. After awhile, Cassidy noticed he was less attentive and seemed to pull away from her. His face was noticeably paler, and he barely touched his plate.

"Are you feeling all right?" she whispered.

Dell snapped back to attention, though the spark was noticeably absent from his blue eyes. He reached over and laid his hand on hers. "I'm fine. Don't worry."

Though she tried not to, she couldn't help worrying. She wanted to suggest he retire for the night but knew he wouldn't. So she said nothing.

The sun was descending in the western sky by the time all traces of supper were put away and the music began. Dell leaned in close, his breath warm on her neck. "Dance with me." Standing, he offered her his hand. "Please."

Her heart beat furiously as she allowed herself to be pulled to her feet. It seemed to Cassidy that she floated into his arms. She pressed her head to his shoulder and felt his lips brush her hair. A warm, cozy feeling engulfed her as she closed her eyes and allowed a sigh of contentment to escape her lips.

Suddenly, she felt Dell stiffen and tighten his hold. Her eyes flew open and she looked up to find him glaring over her shoulder. Turning her head, she spied the wagon master striding toward them while, behind him, a group of snickering men stood watching the scene.

"Time to share the bride's dances, Dell." Lewis said, grinning from ear to ear.

"Thought you were worried about an Indian attack," Dell replied in an icy tone. "Shouldn't you be standing guard or something?" He made no move to relinquish Cassidy.

"Come, now. Be a sport." The amusement on the wagon master's face made his face even redder as he fought to keep from laughing and clapped Dell on the shoulder. "You'll get her back later."

A thrill passed through Cassidy. He didn't want to let her go. "Dell," she whispered, placing a gentle palm on his chest. "I think I'm supposed to dance with the other men. It's okay."

Dell scowled and released her. "I'll be back," he said, eyeing Lewis.

For the next hour, Cassidy was whirled from one man to the next. Each time Dell started her way, another hurriedly cut in before he could get to her. The men laughed and elbowed each other like it was a merry game. All the men except Dell. Cassidy was beginning to agree with her husband. Enough was enough. Close to tears, she had long since stopped trying to converse with her dance partners, when she felt familiar arms encircle her waist. She raised her head to find her husband staring down at her in the flickering light of the campfires.

"Oh, Dell. Thank goodness, it's you."

"Had enough dancing?"

She nodded.

Before she could say another word or think another thought, Dell grabbed her by the hand, without so much as a glance back, and led her to the wagon.

"Dell," she said with a gasp, grabbing his arm for support as he stumbled slightly. "What are people going to say?"

"What does it matter?" He shrugged. "We're leaving the wagon train tomorrow, anyway."

That was true enough. Still, the look of bewilderment on the Pike sisters' faces would haunt her for the rest of her life.

When they reached the wagon, Dell stepped aside and held out his hand. Ducking her head, she climbed inside. When he didn't follow, Cassidy frowned. Maybe she'd been wrong after all.

"I'll leave you alone for awhile," he said.

She gave a slight nod, wondering at the flush in his cheeks.

"But I'll be back," he said softly and closed the flap.

Dell's saddlebags and rifle rested discreetly in the corner of the wagon, and Cassidy felt her cheeks burn. When had he brought those in here?

Her heart raced like a wild horse running free on the range. She was no fool. She knew what Dell expected of her—or she thought she did. Somehow, through the course of this dreamlike day, the stakes had changed. She knew this would be no marriage of convenience.

Lord, how do I give myself to a man who isn't in love with me? It never occurred to her to ask how she would give herself to a man she didn't love, for in the past few weeks, she had fallen for Dell. His fun and humor, the way he played and teased with Emily, who was slowly healing from the loss of her father. Each kind or protective gesture toward Cassidy or the little girl had endeared him to her more. *Dear Lord, let my love for him be enough.*

She removed her gown. Carefully, lovingly, she folded it and packed it into her trunk. Taking a deep breath, she lifted her new white cotton nightgown. With trembling fingers, she removed the rest of her clothing and slipped the gown on. Then she quickly grabbed her wrapper and drew it around her.

Her mind traveled to the four children waiting for her at home. *My children.*

She smiled at the thought. All of them—Dell's four and Emily. She was now mother to five children. How long had she ached and prayed for a family of her own? God had answered her prayers above her wildest hopes. Except for. . . well. . .Dell didn't exactly love her, but he would one day. She felt sure of it. Her God wouldn't leave her in a marriage without love.

❧

Dell sat beside the creek watching the moon cast a gentle glow on the rippling water. His head ached, and he knew he was running a fever. With a groan he placed his hand on his spinning head. He should have been back at the wagon long ago, but he couldn't seem to force his aching body to move.

At first he'd thought it was just nerves—what with the fainting and all. But as the day wore on, he knew he'd caught Emily's sickness. What would he tell Cassidy? Well, she'd probably be relieved anyway. She'd made it pretty clear the marriage was strictly to provide security for her and Emily and to provide a mother for his children. For all intents and purposes, theirs was a marriage of convenience. There were moments though, when he had begun to wonder if perhaps it could be more. The way she'd responded to his kiss and leaned against him during their dance, for instance. He almost believed. . .

Lights were beginning to go out across the camp by the time he summoned the strength to stand, trembling, to his feet and force his legs to move—one, then the other, until he finally reached Cassidy's wagon.

Leaning against the frame, he tapped, hoping it was loud enough for her to hear, for he knew he didn't have the strength to knock any louder.

The canvas flap opened, and there was Cassidy, clad in white, looking very much like an angel, her hair long and flowing around her shoulders.

"Dell, I was about to come looking for you." The unmistakable concern in her voice filled him with contentment.

"Help me inside," he croaked.

"Are you sick?" Cassidy grabbed his arm and pulled as he climbed. Once inside the wagon, he rolled miserably onto the straw bed.

Curling into a ball, he began to shiver uncontrollably. "I–I think I c–c–caught. . ."

"Oh my, you really are sick, aren't you?"

Dell felt a cool, gentle hand on his forehead, then heard her gasp. "You're burning up. Honestly, Dell, why didn't you say something earlier?"

"I didn't want to ruin the day for you."

"That was sweet of you, but if you were sick all day, you should have said something," she scolded. Sliding on her boots, she grabbed a bucket. "I'll be back. Try to get undressed and under the covers."

Dell tried to sit up but fell with a groan to the bed.

Cassidy returned minutes later. She clucked her tongue, and he felt her tugging at his boots. With a grunt, she removed one, then the other. Next he felt his pants sliding from his body. He tried to protest, but she hushed him. "Don't be silly. You can't rest comfortably in trousers."

He didn't protest further as she removed the rest of his outer clothes, and soon he felt a thick quilt covering him to his shoulders. A cool cloth bathed his face. The last thing he heard as he drifted to sleep was the low, melodious sound of Cassidy's voice beseeching God on his behalf.

The noon sun blazed overhead when Dell emerged, pale and shaky from the wagon the next day.

"Feeling any better?" Cassidy asked, looking up from stoking the fire.

"Some." He glanced around at the empty campsite. "Where is everyone?"

Cassidy shrugged and waved a hand toward the westward trail. "Oh they pulled out hours ago."

"Why didn't you wake me?"

The accusing tone caused Cassidy's defenses to raise. "You were in no condition to go anywhere." She placed her hands on her hips. "Now, do you feel up to coffee or breakfast?"

Dell shook his head and placed a hand to his stomach. "No thanks. But we need to get going if we're to make any progress before nightfall."

"You can't go anywhere today."

"We can't stay here on the open prairie like sitting ducks, just waiting to get our scalps lifted." He sounded exasperated. "Didn't you hear Lewis talking about the Indians?"

"Well then, I'll get things packed up, and you can tell me which direction to head," she said firmly, giving him no chance to argue. "But you are staying in bed."

"Emily was over her sickness quicker than this," he complained.

"Well, maybe you should have had Reverend Marcus pray over you last night," she retorted. "But since he's gone, you'd better go back to bed and let it run its course."

Within an hour they were on the trail, Cassidy following Dell's instructions that she just "head southwest." She tied his horse behind the wagon, and Emily skipped alongside. Dell slept through the day, and when they stopped at dusk, Cassidy was relieved to note that his color was returning, though he still refused any food.

The next morning they left as soon as the sun peeked over the horizon. Still weak, Dell allowed Cassidy to drive while he divided his time between lying in bed and sitting beside her on the wagon seat.

In the midafternoon heat, Cassidy came to a rippling creek where a trio of oak trees formed a canopy over the grassy bank. It seemed to her that the trees had been placed there on purpose for weary travelers to rest beneath their branches. Unable to resist the compelling shade, Cassidy pulled the team to the water. She waited while the oxen had their fill, then looped the reins over a nearby bush.

"Can I go swimming?" Emily implored. "I'm so hot."

Cassidy nodded. "For a little while, but we can't stay long."

"Yippee!" Emily quickly discarded her shoes and removed her dress. Clad in only her undergarments, the little girl jumped into the river, splashing with delight.

The water seemed to beckon, and Cassidy hesitated only a moment before removing her own shoes and unbuttoning the top few buttons of her dress. Picking up her skirt with one hand, she waded into the shallow water along the bank. Bending, she scooped water over her throat and chest and the back of her neck.

"Now there's a lovely sight."

Cassidy gasped and whirled around. "Dell! You nearly scared the life out of me."

"I've told you before to be more careful. If I was—"

"I know, I know." Cassidy waved a hand in his direction and turned back around. "If you were an Indian, you'd already have my scalp."

"Exactly." The amusement was evident in Dell's voice.

"You seem to be feeling better," Cassidy observed wryly, scanning the water for Emily. She found the redhead not far from them, bobbing in the water.

"Don't go too far, Em."

"I'm not," the little girl threw back.

"As a matter of fact, I am feeling better." Barefoot, with his trousers rolled up midcalf, Dell had waded through the water and now stood beside her. His gaze roved over her neck, a gleam lighting his eyes.

She felt her cheeks grow hot and quickly buttoned her dress. Cassidy swallowed hard. Slowly, she waded out of the water, with Dell following close behind.

"Time to go, Emily," she called.

"Aw, Ma."

Cassidy's eyes widened and she stared in wonder at Dell.

He grinned. "Well, it seems you have a new title. Better get used to it."

Tears swam in Cassidy's eyes. The honor of being someone's mother was something she could definitely get used to.

Dell reached out and squeezed her hand. "This is cause for a celebration. Why don't we stop here for the night?" he suggested. "We only have a couple hours left before dusk anyway."

"I thought you didn't want to stop for very long during the day," Cassidy reminded. "Seems to me I remember something about 'sitting ducks.' "

"Hmmm. This is a pretty secluded area. We'll just keep a close eye out."

With a shrug, Cassidy consented. "You're the boss."

"Okay, then. Emily stay in that water and splash all you want. We're staying here for the night."

"Yippee!"

Cassidy smiled.

Later during supper, Dell ate ravenously of the catfish he'd pulled from the river. Cassidy sighed. It was good to see him well again.

"Play ball with me," Emily pleaded when the last bit of meat was flaked from the fish's bones.

"Oh, Em," Cassidy protested. "Dell probably doesn't feel up to such activity this soon after his illness."

"Sure I do," Dell replied, hopping to his feet for emphasis and sending Cassidy a broad wink. "Come on, Emily, I'll toss the ball to you for awhile. Then we'll sit here and I'll tell you a bedtime story. Would you like that?"

Emily clapped her hands together. "Yes, please!"

A smile touched Cassidy's lips as the two played. Even her brother, though always a kind father, wasn't as involved with Emily as Dell was already. Cassidy sat in awe at the plan God had laid out before her. Her heart did a little dance. They would arrive at the ranch sometime late tomorrow, Dell had said. Cassidy sighed deeply, thinking of her new home. *Thank You, Lord.* She had thanked God so many times in the last few days that she was sure He was tired of hearing it. Well, not really, but her heart was definitely full of gratitude.

The sun had completely gone by the time the last dish was wiped dry. Dell and Emily had tired of the ball game, and the little girl sat enraptured by the fire, listening to Dell weave a tale about a beautiful mermaid locked away in the lair of an evil sea monster. Cassidy would have preferred hearing about Jonah and the big fish if Dell had to tell a sea story, but she couldn't resist the romantic tale of the mermaid. She sighed audibly when the merprince rescued the young mermaid and whisked her away to his kingdom as his bride, thus ending the story.

Dell glanced her way, lips pursed in an effort not to laugh. Blushing, she snatched up a small twig and tossed it at him. He threw back his head, his laughter ringing in the night air.

With a lift of her chin, she stood. "Come on, Emily. Bedtime."

"Yes, Ma'am," the little girl replied with unaccustomed compliance.

Cassidy glanced at Dell and shrugged. She wasn't going to quibble with a blessing, that was for sure.

After the little girl changed into her nightgown, Cassidy reached over and gave her a kiss on the forehead. Emily grabbed her, pulling her close. "I love you, Ma."

"I love you back, Sweetie. Very much."

"Do you think my pa would get mad if I called Dell 'Pa'?"

Taken aback, Cassidy sat on the edge of the mattress. "I think your pa is so happy that you have such a wonderful man looking after you, he doesn't care what you call him."

"Think Dell would mind?"

"I think Dell would love it, Honey."

Emily seemed to consider the words for a moment, then nodded.

"I guess I probably will, then." she said matter-of-factly. She nodded, and the issue seemed settled in her little-girl heart as she stared up at Cassidy with wide eyes. "Can I say my prayers now?"

Unable to speak past the lump in her throat, Cassidy simply nodded.

Emily bowed her head and was almost asleep before she finished praying.

When she returned to the campfire, Cassidy found Dell lying on his bedroll, hat over his face. He appeared to be sleeping, and relief mixed with disappointment washed over Cassidy.

With a sigh, she strolled the few feet to the river and sat staring out at the reflection of the stars and moon in the perfectly clear night. Gazing at the still, inviting water, she yearned to immerse herself. Impulsively, she stood, removed her dress and undergarments and draped them over a bush. She knew she was alone, still modesty prevailed, and she folded her arms across her chest, while she waded deeper and deeper. Soon, only her neck and head were out of the water.

Eyes closed, she tipped her head back until her hair was fully wet, and the tension began to slacken in her shoulders as a gentle breeze blew across her face. With a contented sigh, she opened her eyes. A silhouette at the edge of the water captured her attention and fear swept through her as her mind replayed Dell's words about the Indians lifting her scalp.

Slowly the figure moved from the shadow of the trees and stepped into the moonlight. Cassidy's heart pounded in her ears as she recognized Dell. His gaze locked onto hers for what seemed like an eternity. Then suddenly, without a word, he turned and walked away.

Cassidy drew a steadying breath and hastened from the

river. Trembling, she dressed quickly and walked back to the campsite to find Dell lounging on his bedroll. Propped on an elbow, he stared into the fire. When she approached, his gaze slid up the length of her before locking onto hers. She shivered, hypnotized by the flicker of the campfire reflecting in his blue, blue eyes.

"Sit," he commanded softly.

Her reply was halting, her voice sounded strange to her own ears. "I. . .have. . .to get the brush or my hair will look terrible."

"Get it."

Once inside the safety of the wagon, she closed her eyes and shook her head in an effort to regain some semblance of control over her emotions before facing her new husband again. Grabbing the brush, she returned to Dell.

"Come here," he said. "Sit by me."

Slowly, she complied, willing her legs to move—first one, then the other—until she reached him. She sat without speaking a word and brushed her ginger tresses until she felt the warmth of Dell's hand cover hers. She turned to face him. The look in his eyes left her breathless.

"Let me," he said softly, taking the brush from her hand. With long, slow strokes he smoothed the silky strands. Cassidy's eyes closed involuntarily, and the contentment she'd felt during the dance at their wedding returned.

"Tell me why you've never married," Dell murmured against her ear.

Cassidy felt herself stiffen. "Because no one ever asked me."

"Why is that?" he pressed.

Pulling away from him, she took the brush. "I think all the tangles are out now. Thanks." She moved toward the safety of the wagon. "I suppose I'll go to—"

"Sleep out here with me," he said, softly.

Her heart jumped into her throat at the melting glance he sent her.

"We haven't had a chance to discuss our new situation," Dell pressed. "I don't expect anything from you."

Cassidy nodded. "I'll be back." Grabbing a quilt from the wagon, she returned to his side.

Dell took the quilt from her and spread it out over the ground.

She sat. Leaning forward, she began to remove her boots.

Dell raised a questioning brow in her direction.

"I just can't sleep with shoes on my feet," she explained.

With a grin, he took the boots and set them aside before dropping down next to her.

"I didn't mean to upset you earlier."

"Please, Dell," she implored. "I just don't want to talk about why no man ever wanted me before—" She cut off the rest of the sentence. After all, he didn't really want her either—he only wanted a mother for his children.

Dell stretched out on the pallet and looked up at her expectantly.

Gingerly, she lay back. His arm crept around her until he pulled her head onto his shoulder. His fingers delved into her hair.

"What's that scent?" he asked, his mouth against her temple, muffling his words. His voice was husky, velvety, and Cassidy's stomach turned over.

"Lilac water."

"Hmm."

"T–tell me about the ranch."

Dell gently removed his arm from beneath Cassidy's head and propped himself up on his elbow. A faraway look came into his eyes and, when he spoke, there was pride in his voice. "We have four hundred acres of grassy fields and three hundred head of cattle grazing on the prairie grass.

Cassidy felt her eyes grow big as he continued.

"I've worked hard to make it what it is. We thrive. My children are well taken care of. . .except for the fact that they haven't had a mother." His gaze roved tenderly over her face.

"Until now, that is."

Dell's eyes traveled to Cassidy's lips, which parted slightly as she drew in a breath. His head lowered until he took her mouth with his own. Trembling, her arm clasped around his neck, and she returned his kiss.

After a moment, Dell pulled away suddenly. "Maybe you'd better go on and sleep next to Emily," he whispered.

With a sudden burst of boldness, Cassidy pulled his head back down. He hesitated for a moment as his eyes searched hers. Seeming to find what he looked for, he closed his eyes and reclaimed her lips.

six

Cassidy woke the next morning enveloped in Dell's strong arms. He stirred as she sat up. Staring down at his handsome face, she drew a deep, steadying breath as the memory of the previous night brought a blush to her cheeks.

Dell opened his eyes and smiled. "Good morning." His voice was low and husky from sleep.

Cassidy's eyes darted to the embers still glowing from the campfire. "Good morning," she whispered, then stood. "I suppose I should get breakfast started."

"Cassidy."

Slowly, she forced herself to meet his gaze.

"You might want these."

Embarrassed, she reached out and took the boots he held.

"Thanks." She turned and rolled her eyes. *Honestly. Can you make more of a fool of yourself, Cassidy Sinclair? St. John, that is.*

"And Cassidy?"

Inwardly, she groaned, but she still turned back to face him. "Yes?"

He opened his mouth, then closed it again, averting his gaze. "Never mind."

Anxiety gnawed at her stomach. "Something wrong, Dell?"

He pulled his own boots on and stood. Coming close, he wrapped her in his arms. "Nothing's wrong," he said. "Everything's right, and I don't want to tempt the fates by saying too much."

Cassidy pressed her head against his shoulder. "I don't believe in the fates. I believe in God and He has been so incredibly good to me." She smiled as his arms tightened about her. "All I've ever wanted was a husband and children."

"You certainly won't be disappointed there. With five young'uns running around, you'll have your hands full," Dell said dryly.

"I wouldn't be disappointed to add a couple more," she replied shyly, feeling her face grow hot again.

Dell stiffened and held her at arm's length. He stared pensively at her for a moment, then dropped his hands from her waist. "You'd best wake Em and get breakfast started while I tend the animals. We ought to be going soon if we're to reach the ranch by nightfall."

A chill settled over Cassidy's heart, replacing the warmth of Dell's arms. What had happened? Disheartened, she headed toward the wagon to rouse Emily.

After breakfast, they quickly loaded their things and were soon back on the trail. Dell rode his horse alongside the wagon, while Emily walked on the other side. Merrily, she waded through the tall prairie grass, exclaiming over the sunflowers towering above her.

Following a well-worn path, they trudged along, a tense silence filling the air between Cassidy and Dell.

"It's almost noon," Cassidy ventured. "Should we find a place to eat dinner?"

Dell shook his head. "My brother and sister-in-law live just a ways further. We'll be there within the hour and can have a meal with them."

"All right." Silence once more permeated the air between them.

Emily played alone, occasionally letting out a delighted squeal when encountering a prairie dog or chicken. When she grew tired, she climbed up into the wagon or rode with Dell.

Cassidy's mind wandered back to the morning conversation with Dell. What had she done? Then it hit her. Dell must not want to have any more children! Cassidy almost gasped at the revelation. Her eyes darted to Dell to see if he'd noticed, but he seemed lost in his own thoughts.

Tears welled up in Cassidy's eyes, though she fought desperately to push them back. Not have children! But her greatest desire was to be a mother, to bear her own flesh-and-blood child. *Oh Lord, what will I do?*

She'd promised to love, honor and obey her husband. God had already met her expectations and even given her more than she'd asked for. He would make a way for her. She had to trust Him.

Caught up in her own thoughts, she jumped when Dell pointed to a small structure ahead of them.

"There," he said, "That's where George and Olive live."

Cassidy's gaze followed his pointing finger, and a bewildered frown creased her brow. "I've never seen such a home before."

He reined in his horse, and Cassidy followed suit with the team of oxen.

With a low chuckle, Dell dismounted and offered her his arms in assistance.

"You'll get used to seeing soddies." He set her carefully on her feet.

"Soddies?"

Dell nodded. "Trees are pretty scarce. Most of the homes you'll see are made of turf."

"Do you mean to tell me that house is made of dirt?"

"That's right." He looked toward the little house. "Anybody home in there?" he called.

A wooden door opened, and a small brunette appeared, wiping her hands on her apron.

"Dell!" He stumbled as she flung herself into his arms. "It's so wonderful to see you." She glanced over his shoulder with a frown, then turned her questioning gaze upon his face.

Dell took Cassidy by the hand. "Olive, I want you to meet my wife, Cassidy. And this," he said, reaching for Emily, who shyly took his other hand, "is Emily, my new daughter." There was pride in his voice. Emily had been trying out the word "pa" all day, much to Dell's delight.

Olive seemed flustered, but recovered her composure quickly. Smiling, she grabbed Cassidy and gave her a tight hug, then repeated the action with Emily.

"It's so nice to meet you both." Her brown eyes twinkled, and she seemed genuinely pleased. "Well, you must be starving. I was just putting dinner on the table. George is clearing the south pasture, but don't worry, he'll be back any time." She threw Cassidy a mischievous wink. "I declare, that man can smell my prairie chicken pie five miles away."

Dell chuckled. "Mind if I take care of the animals?"

Olive waved her hand toward the barn, also made of sod. "Of course, help yourself to feed and water." Turning her attention to Cassidy, she offered a friendly smile. "Come in and rest while I finish putting the food on. You can tell me all about how you two met."

"Excuse me, Ma'am," Emily spoke up. "I need to, that is. . ." Her face glowed bright red.

Olive nodded her head in understanding. "It's around back," she said with a small grin playing at the corners of her mouth.

Emily took off running, and the two women turned back to the house.

Cassidy relaxed as she followed Olive into the soddy. The interior of the rustic home was surprisingly cool, a welcome relief from the hot wind outside.

Curiosity getting the better of her, Cassidy glanced around, hoping she didn't appear rude but unable to stop herself. Rag rugs adorned the earthen floor, in the attempt, she supposed, to give it a more homey feel. A rough little table sat in one corner, but there were no chairs around it. She wondered briefly where they would all sit for the meal. In one corner of the room stood a wood framed bed covered with a patchwork quilt.

The sound of Olive's laughter interrupted her scrutiny. "The first time I saw a soddy, I felt exactly the same way," she said.

Cassidy ducked her head. "I'm sorry, I didn't mean to be rude."

Olive waved her hand. "No offense taken, really." She let out a small giggle. "When Mother and I came out here from Georgia, four years ago, I was appalled by the 'dirt houses.' Oddly enough, though, I've come to see that they are more practical than the cabins made of logs."

"How so?"

"We're snug and warm in the winter and nice and cool in the summer." She removed a large iron skillet from the oven and placed it on the table. "Log cabins let in all the elements. Plus, the Indians can shoot flaming arrows until they run out of fire, but dirt doesn't burn."

Flaming arrows? Cassidy gulped.

"Tell me about you and Dell." The woman moved on as though she'd never mentioned the Indians.

"Um. . ." How did one tell another woman, expecting romantic details, that she'd answered an advertisement?

Thankfully she was spared, as just then Dell made his appearance in the cabin, Emily tagging along after him. Behind them, a stocky, barrel-chested man entered. He was slightly shorter in height than Dell. His hair was completely gray, and he looked much older than his tiny wife. He sniffed the air appreciatively, then broke into a huge grin. "Hmmm, chicken pie." Grabbing Olive, he picked her up off her feet and hugged her. "My favorite." He gave her a loud, smacking kiss on the cheek, then set her gently on the floor.

Olive slapped him lightly on the arm. "Go on, you crazy man," she said, a flush of pleasure coloring her cheeks.

George turned and stepped toward Cassidy, extending a work-roughened hand.

"I'm George," he said with a good-natured grin. "You must be Cassidy. I'm pleased to meet you."

"Pleased to meet you," Cassidy murmured, accepting the proffered hand.

"Well, let's sit and eat this bounty." George said, rubbing his hands together vigorously.

Sit? Sit where? There were no chairs in sight. Her unasked question was answered as George and Dell grabbed food barrels from the corner and placed them around the rustic table.

Emily grinned broadly and hopped up on one of the barrels. Cassidy couldn't resist an indulgent smile at the child. New adventures kept popping up in the strangest places.

Being on the trail worked up a voracious appetite, and they ate ravenously of the delicious pie. After the meal, Olive surprised them with a fluffy marble cake.

"I made it for the church picnic after service tomorrow," she explained, "but I'd much rather share it now to celebrate Dell's marriage to Cassidy."

Taken aback by the generosity, Cassidy smiled. Her heart lurched as Dell's hand covered her own. She looked hopefully into his eyes and found his tenderness had returned. Maybe things would be all right now.

Soon after dinner, Dell pushed back from the table. "Well," he said reluctantly, "we'd better get going."

"Oh, so soon?" The disappointment in Olive's voice echoed Cassidy's feelings.

But Dell was firm. "We need to get going. I've been gone two weeks longer than I intended, and there are so many things to do."

There was a hint of weariness in his voice. Was he still ill? No, more likely just tired, as she was.

Olive nodded in acceptance, and walked them out.

"Thank you so much for the wonderful dinner," Cassidy said, taking Olive's tiny hands in her own. "It was lovely to meet you."

The other woman pulled her close and gave her a quick squeeze. "Dell deserves happiness. Make him happy, and we'll be friends for life," she whispered in Cassidy's ear.

With a nod, Cassidy hugged her back. "I'll do my best."

George grinned and tugged Emily's orange-red braid. "Well, carrot-top, you're my niece now. Be good for your folks."

"Yes, Sir," she replied with a wide grin of her own as he lifted her up in his arms and deposited her onto the wagon seat.

Cassidy watched Olive give Dell a hug and wondered if she was whispering in his ear, too.

To Cassidy's surprise, Dell tethered his horse to the back of the wagon. "Why don't you climb in the back, Emily?" he suggested, pulling himself up to sit beside Cassidy as the little girl complied.

Cassidy handed him the reins, grateful that she wouldn't have to fight the lumbering oxen for awhile at least.

Soon they were on their way, while George and Olive stood waving good-bye.

With one last look at the sod house, Cassidy wondered what she would find when they reached Dell's home.

❧

The sun sank low in the western sky amid a brilliant pink-orange hue as Dell pulled the wagon to a halt. "We're home," he announced proudly.

Cassidy opened her eyes wide at the sight before her. "Oh, it's made of stone." She hadn't meant to speak aloud.

Dell laughed. "Were you afraid you had to live in a little soddy like Olive's?"

"Maybe a little." She smiled up at him.

"The old soddy is over there." Dell pointed to the now-familiar structure a short way from the house. "My foreman lives there now. We lived there for the first couple of years, until I gathered enough sandstone to build the bigger house."

Cassidy turned her attention back to her new home. Wildflowers bloomed in a bed on either side of the stairs leading up to a porch as long as the front of the house. Peeking over the roof from behind stood a windmill. And in the dusk of the evening, a gigantic oak tree cast a silhouette on the barn a few yards away.

The barnyard was surrounded by a wooden fence. A beautiful black mare cantered back and forth, earning the attention a creature so lovely deserved. Her mane, blowing in the breeze, gave her an air of royalty and took Cassidy's breath away.

"That's Abby," Dell said, following her mesmerized gaze.

As if aware of the admiration, the horse stopped at the fence. Then tossing her head, she neighed what seemed like a welcome and resumed her exercise.

Dell smiled. "It looks as though she approves of you, too. She's yours, if you'd like."

A thrill passed over Cassidy. "Do you mean it?"

"If you want her."

"Oh yes, Dell, thank you. She's lovely."

A look of tenderness crossed Dell's features. "You're lovely," he said, squeezing her hand.

She never quite knew how to respond to remarks like that from him. No one had ever told her she was pretty before. She'd heard things like, "With enough sense, you don't need to worry about your looks." And from old Widower Tridell, who owned the mercantile and was always hinting that she should marry his slovenly son, Merv, "You might not be the best looking thing in the world, but you sure were built for hard work and having babies." He'd said it like it was something she should take pride in. Cassidy's cheeks burned just thinking about it.

"Why do you always do that?" Dell asked, dragging her back to the present.

"Do what?" She forced herself to meet him eye to eye.

"Look down and blush if I pay you a compliment."

Cassidy shrugged. "It's a little embarrassing, I suppose."

"Why?"

"Look, Aunt Cass. Puppies!" Relieved by the interruption, Cassidy tore her eyes away from Dell's smoldering gaze as Emily jumped from the wagon and ran to a pack of wiggling, various-colored pups.

"Those are new to the family. I didn't even have a dog when I left." He sounded just a little annoyed.

"Looks like you have several now," Cassidy observed, finding it difficult to keep the humor from her voice as she watched the giggling Emily romping with the tail-wagging lot of them.

Dell let out a chuckle. "Oh well. I brought a couple of new additions to the family, myself." He climbed from the wagon. "Feels good to stretch my legs."

He reached for Cassidy, who went willingly into his arms. "Welcome home, Mrs. St. John." His voice was husky and filled with promise, making her heart lurch.

He released her as the door flew open and a curly-headed tyke ran toward the wagon. "Pa's home!" he yelled. He reached them in no time and jumped into his father's arms. "Pa!"

Dell squeezed the little boy, who in turn, held on for all he was worth. He opened his round, brown eyes and glanced over Dell's shoulder, spotting Cassidy. Pulling slightly away, he whispered, "Who's that?"

"This is Cassidy."

The front door banged open as more children emerged from the house. The two older boys, grinning and gangly, sauntered shyly to their father. He grabbed them both at the same time and gathered them into a bear hug. With the tension of the initial reunion over, all the boys began to speak at once.

"Did you run into any Indians, Pa?"

"Look at the puppies we rescued," said Jack proudly. "Old man Taylor was gonna drowned 'em—hey who's that girl? Those dogs are mine!"

"Did you bring us anything, Pa?" Luke strolled to the wagon and peeked inside.

"As a matter of fact. . ." Moving back to stand beside Cassidy, Dell slipped an arm around her waist and drew her firmly against him.

"Welcome home, Father." All eyes turned toward the house—to the owner of the velvety voice.

This has to be Tarah, Cassidy thought. Her picture, lovely as it was, hadn't done her justice. She stood, one hand holding onto the log rail which framed the porch. Long, coal-black tresses flowed down her back. A frown furrowed her otherwise smooth brow as she glanced from Dell to Cassidy and back to Dell again.

Dell's face lit up. He reached the porch in a few strides and gathered his daughter gently into his arms. "You're even more grown up than when I left, Honey." He held her at arm's length, shaking his head. "What am I going to do with you?"

Tarah blushed. "Oh, Pa."

Dell took her by the hand and led her down the steps. "Come here. There are a couple of ladies I'd like you all to meet."

The girl threw a wary glance in Cassidy's direction, and even from a few yards away, Cassidy was mesmerized by her brilliant violet eyes.

"Oh Father, how wonderful," Tarah said in a voice that Cassidy didn't quite believe. "You've hired a housekeeper. Granny will be so relieved. She's been working herself to a frazzle taking care of the cooking and cleaning, and in her weakened condition, she really needs the help."

Granny?

"Get your claws back in, little cat," Dell said with a chuckle.

"Why, what do you mean, Father?"

Cassidy knew exactly what he meant. The little minx was deliberately belittling her presence.

"And stop calling me 'Father.' " He grinned and tweaked her nose. " 'Pa' will do, like it has for sixteen years."

Dropping his daughter's hand, he came to stand next to Cassidy. Then, throwing a protective arm around her shoulders, he cleared his throat and made his announcement. "Everyone, I want you to meet my new wife, Cassidy. And this little girl," he said, grinning at Emily, "is your new sister, Emily."

Total silence ensued as four pair of eyes stared at Cassidy. Three with hostility, one with rapture.

Jack left Emily with the puppies and ran lickety-split to his father's side.

"Do I got a ma, now?"

"You sure do, Partner." Dell swung his youngest up into his arms and laughed aloud.

"Yahoo!" He wiggled out of Dell's arms. Then stopped short, staring at Emily. "She's my sister?"

"Yes," Dell replied with a confused frown.

The little boy walked back to the puppies and picked up a brown, wiggling ball of fur. He shoved it at Emily, who still sat on the ground cuddling the pups. "Here. This is Warrior. He's my favorite, but you can have him if you want."

Emily glanced in wonder at the warm little treasure in her arms. She buried her face in Warrior's fur and received a lick on the nose. When she looked back up at Jack, her eyes were filled with tears. "Thank you. I've always wanted a puppy, but my pa. . ." She glanced shyly at Dell. "Well, my other pa always said they made him sneeze."

"Aw, it ain't nothin' to cry about." Jack shook his head and gave his father a look of disgust. "Girls."

A lump lodged in Cassidy's throat, and she could see by Dell's glistening eyes that he, too, was moved.

Shyly, Jack made his way to her. "Do you want a puppy, too?" he asked. "We got five of 'em."

"Why don't we let Cassidy settle in first and we can talk about that later," Dell said, ruffling the blond curls. "What do you say, Partner?"

Jack shrugged. "Okay."

Stiffly, Tarah stepped forward and offered Cassidy her hand. "Congratulations," she said. There was pain in her voice as she glanced at Dell. "If you'll excuse me, I have to finish putting supper on the table. Granny's having another bad spell today."

Cassidy frowned. Exactly who was Granny? Not once had Dell mentioned his mother living with them. Not that it mattered, really. Still, it would have been nice to have had some warning.

Sam and Luke followed their older sister's example, shaking Cassidy's hand.

"I'll unhitch the team, Pa," Sam said, his voice quiet and devoid of emotion.

"I'll help him," Luke piped in.

With a frown, Dell watched his three older children make

their polite, but hasty, exits. A thoughtful expression crossed his face, for a moment, then he grinned and clapped his hands together. "All right, the rest of you inside, now. I can smell that fresh-baked cornbread from here, and it's making me hungrier than a grizzly bear." He glanced at Jack and Emily. "Maybe I'll just eat one of these tasty young'uns and save myself the trouble of table manners." With peals of laughter, the children ran toward the house, five little puppies yipping at their heels, while Dell held his arms up in a menacing, bear-like gesture.

He stopped at the entrance and turned, while Jack and Emily bounded through the door. "You coming in, Cass?"

"What about our things?" she asked, motioning to the wagon.

"The boys'll unload for us later. Now are you coming?"

Flustered, Cassidy forced her legs to move forward. "Of course." She smiled, stepping next to him on the porch. "You're a good father. I'm glad for Emily."

Without a word, Dell swung her up in his arms.

Cassidy gasped, throwing her arms around his neck for support. "Dell, put me down!"

"No, Ma'am. I'm not depriving myself of the pleasure of carrying my bride over the threshold."

Dell stepped through the open door. His face was inches from hers, and Cassidy could feel his warm breath growing closer. After placing a soft kiss on her lips, he lowered her gently to her feet and circled her waist, drawing her to him.

"Well, what is this?"

Cassidy jumped back at the harsh words and turned to stare into the hostile eyes of a woman who could only be Granny. The woman stood bent over, supported by a walking stick. Her hair was snowy-white and pinned up perfectly. Her glance swept Cassidy over from head to toe and her nose lifted slightly.

Cassidy felt the urge to step behind Dell, away from the woman's scrutiny.

Dell stepped forward and placed a kiss on the woman's

cheek. "Mother," he said, "I'd like you to meet Cassidy."

Cassidy frowned up at him until he added, "My wife."

The older woman's eyes narrowed to dangerous slits. "You dare to bring another woman into my daughter's home?" Her voice trembled with anger, and she stamped her walking stick on the floor for emphasis. "I won't have it. I tell you I will not have it. You may tell Tarah I will take my supper in my room."

With a disdainful glance at Cassidy, she turned and limped away. The thud of her walking stick hitting the ground with each step was the only sound in the room.

Dell cleared his throat loudly and looked anywhere but at Cassidy.

"Dell? Is there something you forgot to mention?"

"Cass—"

"I believe there is. Let's see, you mentioned four children. One-two-three-four." She allowed herself the dramatization of counting them off on her fingers for him to see. "Yes, I definitely counted four. But wait. You never mentioned a mother-in-law."

"I'm sorry—"

"So if she's your mother-in-law," Cassidy continued, ignoring his apology, "what does that make her to me? My mother-in-law-in-law? Do I call her 'mother,' too?"

"Are you finished?" His voice was tight, and the muscles of his jaw jumped.

Cassidy's heart fluttered. Had she gone too far?

"Yes, I'm finished," she answered, still holding on to the anger in her voice. "For now."

"Good. Let's get you settled in and have supper. We can discuss this later."

"Fine."

"Her name is Ellen, and no, I wouldn't suggest that you call her 'mother.'" he said wryly.

Cassidy threw him a scathing look and went to help Tarah get supper on the table. What in the world had she gotten herself into?

seven

Dell inhaled deeply, taking in the tantalizing aroma of meat roasting in the oven. His stomach grumbled in anticipation. Glad to be home, he released a contented sigh.

He looked around the room, satisfied at the familiarity of his surroundings, then frowned. It looked like the floor hadn't been swept in days, and a layer of dust coated the hearth. Embarrassed that Cassidy should come home to these conditions, he grabbed the broom from the corner and swept it over the wooden floor, then reaching up, knocked down the cobwebs in each corner of the room.

Since his mother-in-law's stroke, the place had desperately needed a woman's touch. Dell shook his head. At sixteen, Tarah should have been able to care for things, but she'd never been made to help her granny. Now he could see that they had done her no favors by indulging her laziness. Grabbing the rag rugs from the floor, he stepped out on the porch and vigorously shook each one until no more dust flew into the air.

"Welcome back, Boss."

Dell glanced up to find his foreman striding toward the house.

"Johnny," he said, inclining his head. "Glad to see you made it home with the supplies. Have any trouble?"

The young man shook his blond head and lifted his shoulders in a nonchalant shrug. "We saw a few Indians here and there, but they left us alone."

"Good. You're lucky they didn't try to steal anything."

"Yep, that's true enough."

"Well, I'll come by and get the supply list from you in the morning."

"Yes, Sir."

A feeling of unease crept into Dell's gut as he watched the young man swagger away. For some reason, Dell didn't quite trust him. He'd only given Johnny the position after Clem, his old foreman, had gotten married a few months before. A young, single man without other responsibilities seemed the logical choice since the other hands had families nearby and lived in homes of their own. It wasn't that he didn't do a good job—he did. But there was an insolence about this newest employee that bothered Dell.

He pushed the troubling thoughts from his mind. Johnny was young. Maybe he just needed a guiding hand. For now, Dell was going to go back inside and enjoy supper with his family.

When he reached the doorway, he stopped. Cassidy stood beside the hearth, her gaze resting on the daguerreotype before her.

"Cass?"

She turned, a frown furrowing her brow. "I don't understand. Why is Olive in this picture with you and the children?"

Dell drew a deep breath. "It isn't Olive."

Her confused frown deepened. "What do you mean?"

"Anna was Olive's twin sister." Why hadn't he told her before?

She set the daguerreotype back on the mantle and drew a deep breath. When she faced him, her eyes blazed with anger and accusation. "Why do you keep letting me find out things the hard way?" she stormed. "Did you think I'd feel threatened by Anna's sister?"

"I don't know." Dell swept a hand through his hair. "Things were so tense between us this morning, I didn't want to add to the problem or make you uncomfortable in their home." He took a tentative step toward her.

Cassidy crossed her arms. "Let's get one thing straight. I am tired of feeling foolish because you conveniently forget to mention certain things to me. From now on, I would appreciate the consideration of your honesty."

She stalked past him, heading for the kitchen, but Dell reached out a hand and caught her by the arm. "Cassidy, wait."

His heart lurched as she faced him, tears pooling in her beautiful green eyes.

"I'm sorry," he said, drawing her into his arms. "I've been selfish and vague. I promise to be straight with you from now on."

Cassidy's arms crept about his neck in a simple gesture of acceptance and forgiveness. Dell tightened his arms, and they stood locked in the comfortable embrace until Tarah's steely voice interrupted them from the doorway. "Supper's ready."

Dell held Cassidy at arm's length, his gaze searching her face. "Is everything all right now?"

She nodded. "Let's go eat."

He blew out a relieved sigh, and they walked arm in arm to the table.

≈

The children monopolized the dinner conversation, filling their father in on all the details of life on the ranch in his absence. Cassidy sat silently absorbing the family atmosphere and dreaming of the day when these children would eagerly share their lives with her as they were now doing with their father.

Tarah remained as silent as Cassidy throughout the meal and spoke only when Sam began to tease.

"A new family's living on the Crowley's homestead," Sam said, eyeing his sister.

"Sam." Tarah's voice was thick with warning.

"They got three sons and all three of them want to court Tarah. But she's smitten with Anthony."

"Samuel St. John, you better hush your mouth right now."

"Calm down, Tarah," Dell admonished with a chuckle. "Your brother's only teasing."

"You always take his side." Tarah jumped up from the table and ran out of the room, tears streaming down her face.

A look of bewilderment spread over Dell's features, and he glanced at Cassidy for support.

She shook her head. "Honestly, Dell."

"What?" His brow furrowed into a deep frown. "Females," he muttered. "Boys, if you're finished with your supper, why don't you get your chores out of the way then unload the wagon."

"Yes, Pa," came the simultaneous reply, and the two bounded out the door.

"And you, Partner," he said to Jack. "You run along to bed."

"Aw, Pa, do I have to?"

"No arguments. Come hug me good night."

"Yes, Pa." Jack stood and hugged Dell, then looked shyly at Cassidy.

She smiled at him, and his face lit up in a wide grin showing pretty white baby teeth. He walked two steps until he stood before her.

"Do you want me to hug you, too?"

Taken aback, Cassidy nodded. "Why yes, I think I'd love for you to do that, Jack." She opened her arms.

The little boy reached up with chubby arms and grabbed her tightly around her neck. She pulled the warm body close, and her heart melted. When he pulled away, his face was glowing. He lifted his chin and planted a wet kiss on her cheek. "G'night, Ma."

Tears sprang to her eyes at his ready acceptance of her place in his life. "Good night, Jack." She reached out and tousled his curly head.

Smiling, he headed to bed.

"Oh, Dell. . ."

"He's a sweet little guy."

Silently, Cassidy nodded and began to clear the table. Looking up, she noticed Emily's head practically in her plate as her eyes drooped shut.

Dell followed her gaze to the weary child, and the corners of his mouth turned up in a tender smile. Pushing back his chair, he went to her and gathered her up in his strong arms.

He planted a kiss on her forehead and brought her around to Cassidy.

"Good night, Ma," the little girl said with a yawn.

"Sleep tight, Sweetie," she said quietly. "Dell, where will Emily sleep?"

"She'll share Tarah's room. Her bed's big enough for the two of them until I can make Em a bed of her own."

"Wait."

He turned.

"Will this be all right with Tarah?"

"She's had her own room for sixteen years," he said with a shrug. "She'll just have to get used to the idea that she isn't the only girl, now."

"I'm sure you know best, but don't be too hard on her if she's upset about it."

Dell gave her a wink. "I promise I'll be kind. I don't want to destroy your faith in my fathering skills." He turned and sauntered down the hallway.

Cassidy smiled after him. She loved her husband and hoped things would go smoothly as the children grew accustomed to her presence in their lives. Her mind riveted to Dell's mother-in-law, and she shuddered involuntarily. The woman had refused to come out for supper, which was fine with Cassidy, but she knew things couldn't continue as they were indefinitely.

Dear Lord, let things work out, and please help me get through the rough times until they do.

She was half finished washing the dishes when Dell returned.

"Well?" Cassidy asked.

"Well what?" Dell grabbed a dish towel.

"How did it go with Tarah?"

"Oh that. She's a little put out, but I think she'll live."

Cassidy sent him a doubtful look, then took the dish towel from his hands.

"I thought I told you I wouldn't have a man working in my kitchen." Cassidy felt her cheeks burn at her bold statement. "I guess this isn't really my—"

Dell took her wet hands in his. "This is your home to care for as you see fit. You're my wife, and everyone will have to get used to it." He bent forward and placed a kiss on her forehead. "But tonight I am going to help you finish these dishes."

"All right," she said with a contented sigh. "But just this once."

They finished cleaning up and had just settled at the table with two steaming cups of coffee when the door opened. Each of the boys came in carrying something from the wagon. For the next few minutes they carried in crates of books and dishes, pots and pans—a few mementoes from Cassidy's home.

"Where do I put her things, Pa?"

Everyone stopped what they were doing, and Dell cleared his throat. Softly he said, "Put them in your ma's room."

"But Pa. . ."

The look Dell gave the boy was gentle but firm. "Your ma's room," he repeated.

Luke ducked his head, but not before Cassidy saw tears glisten in his eyes.

"Come on, Luke. Let's do it." Sam spoke with defeat edging his voice.

"The room's been like a shrine," Dell explained once the boys were out of earshot. "No one has slept in there since. . . Anyway, I had it all opened up a few months ago, so it's ready."

Fleetingly, Cassidy wondered where Dell had slept since his wife's death but knew this wasn't the proper time to bring it up.

Sam and Luke returned a moment later still carrying Cassidy's things. Their faces were ghostly white.

"What's wrong?" Dell asked with a frown.

"Granny won't let us in there."

"What?" Dell bellowed.

Sam's gaze darted to Cassidy, then back to his father. "Granny said no one is sleeping with you in her daughter's bed." His face grew fiery red as he spoke.

Cassidy's heart wrenched for him. How dare that horrid woman put these children in such an embarrassing situation?

Dell's face grew red with anger. "You boys go on to bed. I'll take care of this."

"Yes, Pa."

" 'Night, Ma'am," Sam said, and was echoed by Luke.

"Good night, Boys. Sleep well." She turned back to Dell. "I don't want to cause problems in your home, Dell."

"Nonsense. You're my wife, now, and that bedroom is yours. Sit and finish your coffee while I deal with this."

Cassidy returned to the table and sat while Dell stormed down the hallway. She heard him pound on a door until it opened.

"What do you think you're doing?" she heard him demand.

"This room belongs to my daughter," came the icy reply. "I will not have another woman sleeping in her bed."

"Thunder and lightning, Woman. This is my room, and I'll give it to whomever I choose."

The woman snorted. "Ha. This was never your bedroom. You slept in the lean-to—most of the time," she added pointedly. "Until you broke your promise and killed my daughter. Now you bring another woman to this horrible country and plan to do it again."

Dell's reply was quiet, filled with controlled anger. "You will remove yourself from this room so that my wife and I can retire for the night."

"No."

"Things will change around here whether you like it or not. Cassidy is my wife, and this is where she'll sleep. With me."

Cassidy heard a strangled sob from the woman. Next came the sound of her walking stick hard on the floor, followed by the slamming of a door.

When Dell reappeared, Cassidy tried to pretend she hadn't heard, but she couldn't stop the tears that flowed.

Silently Dell gathered her into his arms, holding her until the tears subsided, then carried her down the hall. When they reached the bedroom, he hesitated briefly at the door.

"Dell?"

His gaze roved her face, until it rested on her parted lips. He lowered his head and kissed her passionately, almost desperately. Cassidy clung to him, and when he pulled away, she was breathless and wide-eyed.

"Cassidy. . ."

She shivered at the sound of her name upon his lips.

Dell stepped inside and kicked the door closed behind him.

≈

Dell awoke long before the sun rose. He stroked Cassidy's silken hair and drank in the sweet scent of lilacs that always seemed to cling to her.

He glanced at his wife, sleeping so peacefully in his arms. She'd given herself to him the last night on the trail—had been so trusting and willing to be his. She had forgiven him so readily each time he'd asked. Dell pressed a kiss to her head, and contentment settled over his heart as she shifted and snuggled in closer to him.

He had hoped for a better welcome for her. What a homecoming it had been! The children were hurt over his sudden arrival with a wife. Had it been a mistake springing his marriage on the family this way? Maybe he should have just hired Cassidy as a housekeeper until they could get used to her. No! He hadn't wanted her as a hired woman. He'd wanted her exactly where she was. In his arms.

Dell closed his eyes but continued to see the pain reflected in the faces of the three older children. He knew Ellen would continue to spew her venomous words but didn't know how to stop it. It wasn't as though he could throw the children's grandmother out to fend for herself. That she blamed him for Anna's death was obvious. Of course, she couldn't blame him any more than he did himself.

With a silent groan, he threw his free arm over his eyes. He'd made such a mess of everything.

Cassidy stirred in his arms and looked up with sleepy eyes. "Everything all right?" she asked, her eyelids already beginning to close again.

"Shh. Everything's fine, Darling," he whispered, placing another kiss on her temple. "Go back to sleep."

Cassidy smiled and within a few seconds, the steady rise and fall of her chest assured Dell she was sleeping again.

Dell closed his eyes, and suddenly Anna's image invaded his mind. He shifted uneasily at the memory of her sad, pain-contorted face as she told him good-bye. A sudden fear gripped Dell. What if Ellen was right and Cassidy died, too?

Involuntarily, his arm tightened about her. Maybe he should settle into the same arrangement he'd had with Anna to avoid that possibility—separate rooms. He cringed at the idea. In the end it hadn't worked, anyway. Anna had found her way into his room one night, and two months later had announced her pregnancy. When Jack arrived, she'd died—because he hadn't kept his word.

Tears clouded his eyes.

But what if God was giving him a second chance to do the right thing? Maybe he had to prove he could keep his word. If he went back to his own room, peace would settle over the house. The children would still have a mother and he would have a wife—for the most part. Eventually Ellen and the children would grow to accept Cassidy's presence and maybe even come to love her.

Sitting up in bed, he breathed a resolute sigh. That was the way it was supposed to be. It had to be what God intended all along. He had no right to be in here with Cassidy.

With an ache in the pit of his stomach, he pulled on his clothes and picked up his boots. Throwing a last look at his sleeping wife, he opened the door and tiptoed down the hall toward the lean-to.

۶۰

A groan escaped Cassidy's lips as the brilliant sun filtered onto her bed, casting its glow into her eyes. Her grumpy demeanor was soon replaced by a happy smile as she remembered where she was.

Casting a quick glance at the other side of the bed, Cassidy felt her stomach sink. Dell was gone already. Why didn't he wake her before he left?

Rising with a stretch and a yawn, she spread the covers over the bed, then dressed in a faded cotton calico dress. The first thing she was going to do once she settled in was use the rest of the material she'd bought in Council Grove and make herself a couple more new dresses. Emily could use a couple too. Cassidy wrapped her hair neatly and pinned it back. She knew Dell liked her hair down, but at thirty-five she wasn't about to try to get by with a schoolgirl's hairstyle. As she put the last pin in place, she heard a light tap on her door.

"Yes?"

The door opened with a creak to reveal Dell on the other side.

"Why did you knock on your own bedroom door, Silly?" Laughing she reached to place a kiss on his cheek.

With a jerk, he pulled away as though she'd pinched him and retreated to a corner.

Stung by the rejection, Cassidy stood immobile, staring at him, filled with questions she dared not ask.

Tortured blue eyes met her gaze.

"What's happened, Dell?"

"I have something to discuss with you."

"Go ahead," she urged.

"This isn't easy, Cass, but I want you to know I believe it's for the best." His words tumbled out. "I'm moving my things into the lean-to." He averted his gaze.

She frowned. "Do you mean you and I are moving to the lean-to?"

"No," his reply was short. "Only me."

"H—have I done something wrong?" Tears pooled in her eyes. "I mean, have I displeased you?"

The compassion on his face made Cassidy cringe. She might not have his love, but she refused to stand for his pity.

Dell strode to her and took her hands. "I think the children will adjust better if I'm not sleeping in the same room with you."

"I don't understand." Cassidy caught her bottom lip between her teeth to stop the trembling. "You're my husband."

"You heard Ellen last night. She won't stop throwing a fit as long as we share Anna's room." His voice pleaded with her to understand. "It'll be too upsetting for the children."

"If it's only that," Cassidy said, relieved, "we'll both move into the lean-to."

He dropped her hands and shook his head. "No. It has to be this way."

Humiliated, she did the only thing she knew to do. Moving around the room, she picked up anything that belonged to Dell and tossed it on the bed. "If this is what you think is best, I'll pack up your things."

"Leave them. I'll come back later," he said softly.

With one last effort, Cassidy followed, and when he turned, they were nearly touching. "Are you sure this is what you want?"

He dipped his head and brushed a painfully gentle kiss on her lips. "I'm sorry, but it'll be better for everyone this way."

❧

"Everyone but me," Cassidy muttered three mornings later, as she reflected on their conversation. Standing in the barn, she buried her head in her horse's mane and sighed. She hadn't allowed herself the luxury of tears when anyone was around. But when she was alone, they came without warning, and she couldn't have stopped them if she'd tried.

"He doesn't want me after all, Abby," she whispered to the black horse.

She'd been a happy bride for two days. Had felt cherished

and hopeful that she could be a good wife and mother. Now it was over. Dell had made it clear she simply didn't measure up to his expectations, and he regretted the marriage. Oh, he'd said it was for the sake of the children, but Cassidy knew better.

Why did You even make me a bride if I was to live my life in loneliness? she cried out to God.

And that woman! How smug she'd been when Dell had walked past Cassidy's bedroom and retired to the lean-to the night after their arrival.

Cassidy led Abby out of the barn and climbed onto her back. She had to be alone, ached to get away from this place of despair. She wheeled the horse around toward the vastness of the range before her and nudged her to a canter.

"Cassidy, wait." Dell's voice rang in the air, clear and firm.

Fighting the impulse to pretend she hadn't heard, Cassidy tugged on the reins until Abby slowed to a walk, then stopped.

"Where do you think you're going?" Dell's voice was clipped.

"I'm going for a ride, obviously," she said, sarcasm dripping from her lips. "I need to be alone."

Dell grabbed the horse's bridle. "You'll have to find your privacy around here."

"Well, what was the point of giving me a horse I can't ride?" Cassidy glared down at him. "Maybe just a way to make you feel better for reducing me to hired help?"

The pain that crossed Dell's face brought instant remorse to Cassidy. If he had grown defensive or been mean back, she could have stayed angry. But he didn't. She had hurt him.

He recovered quickly and stared up at her with glittering eyes. "You can't go off alone on the prairie. Don't you understand anything you've been hearing about the Indians?"

"I don't know. . ." Feeling like an idiot, she twisted the reins in her hands and refused to meet Dell's eyes.

"They're stirred up right now. The Sioux and Cheyenne are burning and raiding all over the territory and kidnaping women and children."

The blood drained from Cassidy's face, and Dell softened. "I haven't heard of any raids close by, but please be careful." He placed a gentle hand on her leg. "I don't want to lose you."

Warmth from his fingers spread through Cassidy's leg and down her calf. How could he even say something like that when he'd moved out of her bedroom the morning after carrying her over the threshold? And how could he seem so sincere saying it?

She covered his hand with one of her own. "You won't lose me, Dell." A sadness welled up inside of her and suddenly, she felt very tired. "At least not to Indians."

"Cass. . ."

A sob caught in her throat, nearly choking her as she grabbed the reins with both hands and turned Abby toward the barn.

Once inside, she dismounted and unhooked the saddle. As she started to lift it off of the horse's back she felt strong arms behind her, caging her in. *Dell?*

"Hey, now, you shouldn't be unsaddling your own horse." The voice was smooth as honey and definitely not her husband's.

Cassidy wheeled around, coming face to face with Johnny Cooper, the ranch foreman. Ducking under his arms, she glared at him.

"What do you think you're doing?" Anger boiled inside of her. "Don't you ever put your hands on me again."

"Whoa, now," he drawled. A lazy smile played at his sensuously full lips, but his eyes glittered dangerously. "No disrespect intended." Leaving the saddle, he sauntered toward her.

Defenses alerted, Cassidy retreated a step for each step he advanced until her back came up against the barn wall. He was so close, she could see the flecks of gold in his hazel eyes. "Don't come any closer or I'll scream," she whispered hoarsely, fearing she might do just that any second.

He shrugged. "Go ahead, no one will hear you. All the

hands are rounding up cattle. Seems a few were rustled during the night." His voice was calm, non-threatening, but fear gripped her.

"What do you want?" she asked, despising herself for being a coward.

He placed a hand on the wall on either side of her head. "Rumor has it the boss is sleeping in the lean-to."

Horror filled Cassidy. The entire ranch knew of her humiliation?

Johnny took a strand of loose hair between a thumb and forefinger. Leaning in close enough so that Cassidy could feel his breath hot on her face he whispered, "I just thought you might be lonely."

Mustering up her courage, she placed her hands flat against his chest and shoved as hard as she could. Surprise, then anger registered in his eyes as he landed hard on the barn floor.

"Like I said," Cassidy warned through clenched teeth, "don't ever touch me again."

Shaking with anger and fear, she stormed out of the barn and toward the house, only to find Dell walking through the door and strolling her way. So he would have heard her scream after all? Not that he would have cared.

"What's wrong?" he asked.

"Nothing. Just leave me alone."

"Don't be this way. I had hoped we could be—"

"Friends?" Cassidy spat. "Spare me, please. I've heard the 'let's be friends' routine before. Of course, I've never heard it from my own husband."

Leaving him standing with a bewildered expression on his face, she entered the house. She stomped down the hall to her bedroom, only to find Ellen inside with the wardrobe wide open. What next?

"What do you think you are doing in my room?"

The woman turned. "I'm looking for my daughter's shawl. It isn't among the other things I removed from here." She didn't even have the grace to be embarrassed at getting caught or apologetic for the intrusion.

"Well, if I find it I'll let you know," Cassidy said through gritted teeth. "Now please leave. I'd like some privacy."

"Oh? Trouble already?" A look of triumph leaped into the dull gray eyes. "Dell is a self-centered, difficult man, as my Anna discovered much too late. It looks as though you are discovering it as well."

A tiny satisfied smile tugged at the thin mouth, and she limped from the room with the ever present thud of her walking stick ringing in Cassidy's ears.

&

Cassidy poured a steaming kettle of water into the half-filled tub on her bedroom floor. She had waited all day for night to fall so she could have the privacy of a nice, warm bath and a good cry.

Two weeks had passed since Dell had moved into the lean-to. Rather than help the situation as he thought it would, the three older children were openly hostile. Cassidy felt more alone in this house full of people than she'd ever felt in her life.

She lifted her leg over the side of the tub and stepped down. As her foot touched the bottom, Cassidy frowned. Reaching into the water, she ran her hand over the bottom. Rocks! Those little hooligans had put rocks in her bath water. It couldn't have been Jack. He loved her. And it was beneath Tarah to pull such a silly prank. It had to have been Sam and Luke.

With a huff, Cassidy snatched up the basin beside her bed and scooped the rocks from the tub. When she settled back into the now lukewarm water, a few pebbles remained and gouged her bare flesh. Miserable, she hugged her knees to her chest and wept bitterly.

In one dreadful day, all of Cassidy's dreams of marriage and family had been dashed. "Why did You betray me, Lord?" she whispered, knowing even as she prayed that God hadn't betrayed her, she had deceived her own heart. Her desperation to marry and provide a stable home for Emily had compelled her to join herself to a man who, admittedly, had hardened his heart against God.

Oh, Lord, forgive me, please, her heart cried. In marrying outside of God's plan for His people, Cassidy knew she'd become one with a man in clear rebellion. How could she have ever believed God would bless the union? Cassidy shook her head, a strangled sob tearing at her throat. She had been so blind.

What do I do now? Should I take Emily and leave? Immediately, her ravaged heart spoke the answer. Standing before God, she had promised to love, honor, and obey Dell. Now God expected her to carry out her vows—for better or worse. Dell's rejection knifed through her heart until the pain was almost more than she could bear. But worse still, he had rejected God.

Help me not to be bitter against my husband. I don't want to cause him to pull further away from us both.

eight

"I'm not going." Tarah tossed her head in defiance and folded her arms. "I'm too old to sit in school with a bunch of children."

Cassidy lifted her hands in surrender. "All right, I don't suppose I can force you since your pa's gone. But if you stay home, you'll help me around the house."

"You can't make me do anything I don't want to do," Tarah said with a sniff. "After all—"

"I know." Cassidy rolled her eyes and handed out lunch pails to Luke and Sam, then set about making lunches for the girls. "I'm not your mother. So you've said, more than once."

The last four months had been a tug-of-war between the two of them. If Cassidy wanted Tarah to go one way, she went another. Most upsetting was that the girl didn't even try to hide it, especially during the last couple of weeks since Dell had taken some cattle to sell in Abilene.

"Well," Cassidy replied with a shrug, "I assume if you don't want to go to school anymore, you probably intend to marry and care for a home."

Tarah blushed but eyed her suspiciously.

Ah, so I'm right. She does have a beau.

"How do you plan to do that without learning how? Taking care of a home requires some training. It certainly doesn't come naturally."

Placing her hands on slender hips, Tarah huffed indignantly. "I took care of this family while Pa was away marrying you."

"I don't know," said Cassidy dubiously. "It took me a week to get this place to shine when I first came. My muscles ached for days." Well, maybe not that long.

A look of indecision crossed Tarah's features. "Maybe I

don't know all there is to keeping house," she said, with more humility than Cassidy had ever observed in the girl. "But I'll learn."

Cassidy softened. "I could teach you, if you'd let me."

The moment was broken by a stomp of a small boot on the wood floor. "If Tarah isn't going," announced Emily, "then I'm not either."

Now she was outgunned by both willful girls. Cassidy shook her head and looked pointedly at Tarah. For all of Tarah's hatefulness toward Cassidy, she was Emily's hero. Surprisingly, the sixteen year old hadn't balked about sharing her room. Cassidy suspected it was because she identified with the little girl's loss of her mother.

Tarah scowled. "Em, you have to go to school. Do you want to grow up to be an idiot?"

"No, but I don't want to go without you," she said, eyes filled with pleading. "I won't know anyone."

"Oh, honestly."

"Maybe you could go just this first week until Emily adjusts to a new school," Cassidy suggested casually. "It would be a big help."

Tarah grabbed their lunches from the table and shoved Emily's into her hands.

"All right. But just this week."

With a sigh of relief, Cassidy watched the four older children set off for town two miles away.

The township of Harper boasted a little sod schoolhouse which would serve as a church as well as a school once they found a preacher willing to stay. So far, services were held only when the circuit rider came through every few months.

The teacher had arrived just the week before and would take turns boarding with the families in the community. Thankfully, there were enough families to house her for the three-month term, so that she wouldn't need to stay at the ranch. Cassidy couldn't have stood the humiliation of yet another woman knowing about her living arrangements.

As she headed toward the kitchen, a small sigh from Jack brought her up short.

"What's wrong, Honey?"

The little boy still sat at the table, his chin jammed onto one chubby palm. "I don't see why I can't go to school, too. Pa says I'm smart."

A smile lifted the corners of Cassidy's mouth. "Your Pa's right, of course. But who's going to watch out for Warrior if you go to school all day?"

A frown creased his brow as he considered her words.

"By the time you're old enough for school," Cassidy pressed on, "Warrior won't need quite as much attention as he does right now."

"I guess you're right." He stood and gave her a bright grin. "Think I'll go find him so he doesn't get into trouble."

"I think that's a smart idea."

He beamed up at her and took off out the door calling for the pup.

Cassidy grinned and shook her head, then turned her mind back to the task at hand. Stepping into the kitchen, she glanced around at the mess. She had postponed the cleaning up until after the children were off to school and was now faced with a pile of dishes to wash. With a heavy sigh, she took the dishpan from its peg on the wall and set it on the counter. Grabbing the fresh bucket of water from the corner, she filled the basin and picked up a dirty plate.

Her stomach turned at the sight and smell of the dried egg yolk crusted on the dish, and she fought to keep from vomiting in the fresh water. She quickly realized it was a losing battle and, dropping the dish, bolted. Rushing through the kitchen door, practically knocking Ellen over as she did, Cassidy ran outside. Bending over the porch rail, she retched violently until she lost every last bit of her breakfast.

She felt a cloth being pressed into her hand and looked up in surprise to find Ellen standing beside her.

"Thank you," she said, wiping her mouth.

"So, he's done it to you, too."

Wearily, Cassidy sank onto the porch and leaned her head against the rail, fighting a wave of dizziness. "What do you mean?"

"Are you that foolish?" Ellen laughed without humor. "I've watched your bouts of sickness for three months, waiting for you to figure out your condition."

"Do you mean. . .?" She grabbed the woman's gnarled hand. "Ellen, do you think I'm with child?"

She shrugged, pulling her hand away. "What else?"

"Oh, Lord, thank You," Cassidy prayed, unmindful of the woman standing over her.

"I hope you're still thanking Him when the time comes," Ellen replied with a snort, then turned and limped back into the house.

With a sense of wonder, Cassidy placed a tender hand on her stomach. "Hello, little one," she spoke softly, her heart filling with love for the unborn child. "So you're the reason I've been sick and haven't had my—"

In spite of herself, Cassidy felt her face grow warm. Curiously, it had never occurred to her that pregnancy might be the reason she'd failed to have her woman time the past couple of months. She'd been afraid she was passing the time for childbearing. The thought had filled her with dread and despair.

Now she felt indescribable joy and relief. With a gasp, she stopped basking in the joy of her discovery. Anxiety wrapped around Cassidy's heart as she wondered how to tell her husband the news. Given the circumstances, he wouldn't be happy. Well, she just wouldn't tell him for now. She didn't want anything to spoil her happiness.

Cassidy remained on the porch for awhile, reveling in the knowledge of the little secret growing inside of her. Finally, with a sigh, she remembered the pile of breakfast dishes awaiting her. Standing on still trembling legs, she made her way through the door and to the kitchen. She stopped short in surprise at the sight that greeted her. Ellen stood over the counter, drying the freshly washed dishes.

Too stunned to speak, Cassidy stood dumbly in the doorway.

Glancing over her shoulder, Ellen grunted when she spied Cassidy. "I won't have you overworking yourself and leaving those children motherless again." Her voice broke slightly. "I'll take over some of the household duties."

"Thank you for your kindness, but I think I'm fine now. You mustn't overdo it," Cassidy said, gently, stepping into the kitchen. "I couldn't let you—"

Ellen lifted a hand in silence. "I wasn't here for my daughter and she died. If I had been, I could have spared her some of this backbreaking work, maybe even saved her life." Her eyes were tortured. "It's no secret that I am not happy to have another woman in the house, but I can't deny you've been good to me. Please, I need to do this," she finished, barely above a whisper, her tone almost pleading.

"Then at least let me make us some coffee and we can sit together and talk. Maybe it's time we got to know each other."

With only a moment's hesitation, Ellen nodded.

Cassidy went about making the coffee while the older woman limped to the table and sat.

As the water boiled, Cassidy sliced some bread and took down a jar of strawberry preserves. Now that her stomach had settled, she found herself ravenous. She placed the bread, preserves, and two steaming cups of coffee on a tray and walked to the dining area to join Ellen.

Lord, please let us become friends. It'll make things so much easier on the children—and myself.

"Here we go." With a smile, she set the tray on the table.

"Thank you," Ellen said stiffly, accepting the cup of coffee.

They sat in uncomfortable silence for a moment until Cassidy found a common topic of conversation. "I met Olive and George on the way here."

From the hungry look on Ellen's face, Cassidy could see she'd chosen the right subject.

"How is my daughter?"

"She seems well. As a matter of fact, I found her delight-ful. She and George have a cozy little home."

Ellen's face darkened. "She should never have married that man only five years after Peter's death."

"Peter?"

"Her husband. He was killed in the war."

"I–I had no idea."

A faraway look came into Ellen's eyes. "I thought we were doing the right thing by moving here to help Dell care for the children. Peter was gone the first year of the war, and my husband soon after." There was bitterness in her voice as she continued. "The Yankees burned our plantation to the ground when they came through. We lived in the overseer's house until I received word of Anna's death. With my husband gone and the house burned and most of our friends worse off than we were, there was no reason to stay in Georgia. So here we are."

"How awful for you. I'm truly sorry."

Ellen continued as though Cassidy hadn't spoken. "The worst part about it was that Anna didn't have to die. If Dell had just left her alone. . . She was small and delicate, like Olive, and shouldn't have carried one child, let alone four. Dell knew that, but he didn't seem to care."

Resentment welled up within Cassidy at the criticism, but unwilling to lose her newfound ally, she said nothing.

A tear rolled down Ellen's wrinkled cheek. "And now the same thing will happen to Olive."

"I don't know," Cassidy soothed. "Olive seems pretty robust to me."

Ellen's hand came down hard on the wooden table top. "It's this country! This wretched land. It's harsh and unyield-ing for women. We work and work until finally we die, one way or another."

Ellen's thoughtful gaze scanned Cassidy's face, then moved down to her stomach. She drew a breath. "I rattled on too long. You must take care of yourself and stay strong."

Cassidy's mind was reeling from the woman's outburst. Still, her eyes felt heavy as a wave of fatigue swept over her.

"I am tired," she admitted.

"Then you must go and lie down."

With a nod, Cassidy stood and reached to pick up a dish.

Ellen placed a restraining hand on her arm. "I'll just finish my coffee and clean up this mess."

Cassidy hesitated, then nodded. "All right," she said. Making her way to her bedroom, she stopped and turned. "Many women thrive on the prairie and bear children who thrive as well. I am so very sorry for the loss of your daughter. But you mustn't blame Dell or yourself for her death."

Ellen stared silently at the cup in her hands.

"I'll be going, now," Cassidy said softly. "Thank you for your kindness today."

≈

Dell reined in his roan mare and dismounted. After two weeks away from home, he was ready for a hot meal, a bath and a comfortable bed.

"Take care of my horse, will you, Johnny?" he asked, slinging his saddlebags over his shoulder.

"Sure, Boss."

They had gotten a good price for the cattle—enough to last the winter. This had been the most profitable year so far for the ranch, and he'd splurged on little surprises for his family. Anxious to pass out the gifts, he sauntered toward the house, grinning in anticipation. He expected the door to burst open any moment and five happy children to run out to greet him. When the door remained shut, he frowned, wondering where everyone could be.

He opened the door slowly and stepped inside. "Hello!" he called.

"For pity's sake, be quiet. You'll wake Cassidy." Ellen sat in the wooden rocker before the fireplace, knitting in her hands. Something Dell hadn't seen her do in months.

"Mother, it's good to see you feeling well enough to be up

in your chair." He glanced around. "Where are the children?"

"Jack is napping. The others are at school."

"Oh, good, the new teacher arrived, then." Dell deposited his dusty saddlebags on the table. Receiving a scolding frown from Ellen, he snatched them back up and swiped at the dust on the table. He tossed the bags into a corner. "I'll get those out of the way soon as I get something to eat."

"There's some bread, already sliced, wrapped up on the kitchen counter and some preserves in the cupboard. And don't make a mess."

Dell's eyebrows shot up, wondering what had brought about such a change in his mother-in-law. Rather than question her, he decided to count his blessings and let it go.

He grabbed the bread and took it to the table, devouring it ravenously, without the preserves. "Everything okay while I was away?"

"Of course," Ellen replied tersely. "Why wouldn't it be?"

"Did you say Cass is sleeping?" Concern filled him. "She sick?"

Silence filled the air long enough that Dell thought maybe she hadn't heard him. He was about to repeat the question when she spoke up.

"Cassidy needs rest. She does twice as much around here as anyone in the house and just got herself tired out. She'll be fine, but she needs to slow down some."

Concern turned to fear as a gnawing sensation crept through his midsection. "What do you mean?"

"Just what I said." Annoyance sharpened her tone. "You've got to get her to rest more."

If Ellen was concerned about Cassidy, something had to be wrong.

"Mother, just tell me if Cassidy is ill."

"Didn't you hear what I said? She needs more rest, that's all. Make her rest. And she especially needs to stay out of that garden during the heat of the day."

Dell lifted his arms in helpless appeal and let them drop to his knees. "Then what do you suggest I do?" He wished she would stop rocking and knitting and just look at him.

As if she'd read his thoughts, she sat still in the chair and gave him a steady gaze. "It might not hurt to have a little fun around here. Things have been rather dismal since you brought her, through no fault of her own, I might add."

Dell squirmed like a young boy who'd been caught doing something wrong, and he found himself wishing she would go back to her rocking and knitting. Something had most certainly happened while he was away. He never thought he'd see the day Ellen would champion Cassidy.

Ellen shrugged, resuming her knitting. "A late summer picnic down by the creek wouldn't be a bad idea. The children would love it, and the relaxation would do Cassidy some good."

Actually, it was a wonderful idea. Dell stood and closed the distance between them. Bending, he gave her a peck on the cheek. "You're a genius."

She jerked her head away as though the kiss had defiled her. "Do not think I can be charmed the way the younger women can, Dell St. John. I see you for the selfish man you are. You as good as killed my Anna and now you're doing the same thing to—" She stopped abruptly and returned with a vengeance to her knitting.

With a shake of his head, Dell returned to the saddlebags, reached down, and grabbed them. Strolling down the hall, he reached inside one of the bags and withdrew a small package. He tapped lightly on Cassidy's door and, when he received no answer, gently pushed it open. His heart lurched at the sight of her sleeping soundly on the bed they had shared one night. With effort, he pushed the image away.

With a frown, he examined her face. Ellen was right. Cassidy was overworking herself. She was pale, and dark smudges colored the skin below her eyes. His heart nearly stopped as she stirred, turning to one side. He laid the package on the bureau, wincing as it made a crinkling noise, and slowly backed out of the room.

&

"Ma!"

Cassidy jolted awake as Emily burst through the bedroom door.

The young girl bounded onto the bed, jostling Cassidy. "I love school! Miss Nelson is just beautiful and so nice." Emily threw her arms around Cassidy and held tightly. "She said I was real smart, Ma."

Returning the embrace, Cassidy breathed a relieved sigh. The little girl had adjusted to her new home better than Cassidy had dared hope. There was an immediate rapport between Jack and Emily, and Tarah had taken her new sister under her wing. Emily adored Sam, and laughed uproariously at Luke's antics, thus endearing her to the ornery boy.

"Sweetheart, I'm so glad you had such a nice day."

Emily wiggled free and sat staring with rapture on her face.

"Did you make any new friends?"

Her braids bobbed as she nodded vigorously. "Becky Simpson is my age, too. She just moved here last month and didn't know anyone either, so we decided to be best friends. Her pa's the new doctor. Miss Nelson said she was real smart, just like me."

It appeared the teacher was not only beautiful and nice, but pretty smart, herself. Cassidy smiled.

Emily hopped off the bed. "I have to go say hi to Pa."

Pa?

"Wait, Em. Dell's home?"

"Uh-huh," the little girl answered as she ran from the room.

Cassidy's heart fluttered. She stood up and smoothed the quilt back over the bed. Walking to the bureau, she grabbed her comb and started to run it through her hair, but she stopped short as her gaze fell on a small brown package.

Realizing it could only be from Dell, she picked it up with trembling hands and carefully opened the gift. Lilac water. Tears welled in her eyes and rolled down her cheeks. He had bought her lilac water. He must have noticed she had run out a while back.

Is there hope after all, Lord?

She placed a tender hand on her stomach. "You have a wonderful pa, little one." she whispered. "I only hope. . ."

Dell was such a good father, but had made it clear he didn't want more children.

A smile played at the corners of her lips. It was too late for that now. Their child was growing right now inside of her, and he would just have to get used to it. That is, when she got up the nerve to tell him.

nine

Squeals of delight greeted Cassidy as she stepped into the sitting room a few moments later.

"Ma, look what Pa brung me," shouted Jack. He was dressed in a war bonnet, long enough to drag on the floor. With a war whoop good enough to put any Indian to shame, he bounded out the front door. Seconds later, the sound of squawking and clucking confirmed he was wreaking havoc on the unsuspecting chickens scratching in the yard.

Dell stood from his place next to the front window and observed Cassidy, his brow creased in an anxious frown. "Here, come and sit," he said, holding onto the back of the wooden chair. "You're still peaked."

Cassidy moved to the seat and lowered herself. "Thank you," she murmured, flustered by his closeness.

"You smell of lilacs again," he said softly.

"Yes, thanks, it was thoughtful of you to realize I was out of my favorite scent."

"It's my favorite scent, too." His low voice brought a shiver up and down her spine. "I've missed it."

Sam cleared his throat loudly. "Thanks for the new rifle, Pa," he said. "Maybe you and me can go huntin' Sunday."

Dell shook his head. "We have plans for Sunday, Son."

Everyone stopped and stared at him curiously.

"What plans?" asked Tarah.

"We're going on a picnic down by the creek." He threw a wink at Ellen, who frowned and rocked harder in her chair. "Your Granny, here, thinks we need a little family fun, and I'm inclined to agree." He glanced around the room, eyeing each of the children sternly. "We've been a bunch of old sourpusses too long. We're going to pack us a lunch and take a ball to play with and maybe even take a dip in the creek or go fishing."

"Hey, I can try out the new rod you brought me!" said Luke. Then his face darkened. "Aw, we can't go Sunday."

"Why's that?" Dell asked with a frown.

"The preacher's going to be in town this Sunday," Luke said with unconcealed disappointment. "Mr. Anderson came to the school today and told us to tell our folks."

Cassidy's heart skipped a beat. A real church service. She'd had no fellowship with believers since they left the wagon train. The thought thrilled her to the very core of her being.

"That's right," Tarah confirmed.

Dell's face clouded over. "Well, thunder and lightning," he muttered with a tentative glance at Ellen. "I suppose you'll be wanting to go to the service?"

"Naturally."

"We'll make it another time, then." Disappointment edged his voice. "I'm going to get cleaned up before supper."

Silence descended upon the room as he made his way down the hall to the lean-to.

"Aw, Granny," Sam spoke up, "couldn't we just skip the service?"

"Certainly not, young man. Sunday is the Lord's day, and if He has seen fit to bless us with a preacher, we will not dishonor Him by going on a picnic instead. Now go do your chores."

"Yes'm," he replied, meekly.

Cassidy's heart went out to the group of disappointed children. After all, they hadn't grown up with church services. A picnic sounded like just the thing to cheer them up.

Suddenly, an idea came to her. "Maybe we could prepare everything Saturday night and have the picnic after church."

All pairs of eyes turned to Ellen in question.

"Well, I suppose that would be all right," she said grudgingly. "As long as we honor the Lord first."

The children let out a cheer. If Granny said it was okay, then it was settled.

An unbidden quiver of resentment welled up inside Cassidy. She was their mother, after all. Granted, not in the natural sense, but she was in her heart. They shouldn't have to ask their grandmother's permission to do something she suggested. She squelched the irritation with a sigh of resignation. Maybe in time.

&

The rest of the week passed in a whirl of activity. The children left for school each day filled with excitement. Emily just "loved" her teacher and had found a kindred spirit in her little friend, Becky.

Tarah seemed to enjoy school, as well, and brought homework to complete each night. She didn't mention their agreement about school, and Cassidy hoped the girl would forget all about quitting school and continue her education. Sam, from what Cassidy had gathered from Tarah's teasing, was smitten with the new doctor's older daughter, Camilla Simpson, Becky's sister. And true to his mischievous self, Luke had placed a bent nail on Randall Scott's chair and had been sent to the corner, not once, but twice during the week. He was severely scolded by his Pa, who warned it would be a trip to the woodshed next time.

For Cassidy, the week was filled with the wonder of her pregnancy. More than once, she'd been tempted to reveal her secret to Dell, but he'd been withdrawn and sullen again after the news of the preacher coming through the area. So she enjoyed her secret in silence, hoping Ellen wouldn't tell Dell before she found the right time to do it herself.

Saturday night, Ellen, Tarah, and Cassidy quickly cleared away the supper dishes and went about preparing their picnic lunch for the following afternoon. Dell had slaughtered two chickens earlier in the day, and Ellen cut them into pieces, then fried them to a golden brown. Cassidy carefully shucked and boiled a mound of corn, still on the cob, then mixed together a batch of corn muffins. Tarah completed the feast by baking a fluffy white cake, marbled with brown sugar and cinnamon.

Once the children were settled into bed, Cassidy stepped onto the porch to escape the heat of the kitchen. Catching a cool breeze, she lifted her head slightly and closed her eyes. A feeling of contentment swept over her as she thought of the family God had given. True, it wasn't what she'd always planned, but she wouldn't trade it for anything in the world. "Lord," she breathed, "thank You so much for the blessings You've brought to my life."

A short laugh startled her, and her eyes flew open. Turning, she spied Dell strolling toward her from a shadowy corner of the porch.

"Honestly, Dell," she said, a hand to her breast. "You scared me half to death."

"You were completely oblivious. What if I'd been an Indian?"

"Would you stop bringing that up? No Indian is going to sneak up on me while I'm standing on my own front porch."

"You never know." Dell shrugged. He stared intently into her eyes. "You were thanking God for your blessings. Did you mean it?"

Cassidy's mind flew to the child growing inside of her and joy filled her.

"Oh, Dell, I'm so happy; happier than I ever thought possible."

A sense of glee washed over her at Dell's stung look. Well, admittedly, she could be happier. But it was Dell's decision that they live apart, and she was tired of moping around about it. She wouldn't fight him anymore or be angry with him. For the children's sakes, she would try to give them a natural happy home, even if things weren't natural and happy between their father and herself.

"Will you come to the service with us in the morning?" she asked.

"No." The answer was clipped, meant to end the subject, but Cassidy felt compelled to press.

"It would mean a lot to the children. . .and me."

Dell's expression softened. He reached out his hand and

brushed lightly at her cheek.

Cassidy closed her eyes. He hadn't touched her like that in so long, she'd almost forgotten how gentle his hands could be upon her. A gentle sigh escaped her lips.

"Cass," he said, his voice husky and low. He stepped forward, claiming her lips with his own.

Cassidy responded with a fervor to match his. *Oh Lord, please!* She loved her husband and wanted him back where he was supposed to be.

Dell groaned and tore his lips away. "Go inside," he said softly. After a last tortured glance, he walked down the porch steps and headed for the barn.

With a sigh of resignation, Cassidy went back inside. She paused at the boys' bedroom and glanced in. Three angelic sleeping faces greeted her. She paused for a moment, watching them, then closed the door lightly. Next she checked on the girls and found Emily sound asleep, while Tarah sat propped against the headboard, reading a book.

"Good night, Tarah," she said softly.

The girl looked up, resentment in her eyes.

"I wouldn't stay up too late," Cassidy ventured. "We have a busy day tomorrow."

"I'm fine."

Cassidy shrugged. "Good night then."

She stepped inside her empty bedroom and wearily changed into her nightgown.

Reaching up, she removed the pins from her hair and shook her head, letting the tresses cascade down her back. She gave her hair one hundred strokes, then stood. Making her way to the inviting bed, she pulled back the covers. A gasp escaped her lips as a black snake, free of the confining quilt, slithered from her bed and onto the floor. An ear-piercing scream tore at her throat before blackness claimed her.

❧

"Cassidy, Darling, wake up."

From far away, Cassidy heard Dell's voice breaking

through her foggy mind, and slowly she opened her eyes. Dell sat on the floor, cradling her in his arms, while her head rested on his lap. The three older children stood around them, taking in the scene.

"What happened?" Dell asked.

"S–snake." She gulped.

"Snake?"

"There was a snake in my bed."

"How in the world would a snake have gotten into your bed?" Dell wore a perplexed expression on his face.

"I don't know," she said, her head beginning to clear. "Why don't you ask the snake?"

How indeed? Cassidy sat up and glanced around at the faces of Sam, Luke, and Tarah. She was a little surprised to find Tarah's eyes clouded in concern. The boys were red faced, and lowered their heads at her scrutiny.

Ah-ha. Those little. . .

Sam glanced up and caught Cassidy's knowing gaze. He cleared his throat.

"Uh, Pa," he said slowly.

Cassidy broke in quickly. "Dell, I'm sure it just came in and found it's way to my bed accidentally. I've heard of things like that before."

Now why had she defended those little hoodlums? They certainly deserved the whipping Dell surely would have given them.

The looks on the boys' faces as they looked from her to each other registered surprise that matched her own.

"Well, I'll take a look around and see if it's still here," said Dell, helping her to her feet. "Boys get back to bed."

"Uh, sure Pa."

"You too, Tarah. And snuff out that candle. It's bedtime."

"Yes, Pa. 'Night."

Cassidy sat quickly on the bed and pulled her legs off the floor. She was sure she heard laughter coming from the hallway as the boys made their way back to their room. She almost wished she hadn't defended the ungrateful pair.

Dell scanned the room, then looked in every corner and drawer, as well as through the wardrobe.

To Cassidy's relief, the snake appeared to have taken its leave.

"Well," he said, scratching his head, "I still don't know how it could've gotten in here, but I guess it left the way it came."

He glanced at Cassidy, a concerned frown creasing his brow. "You going to be okay?"

She nodded, still trembling from the ordeal.

Dell hesitated. "I could stay for awhile."

"That's not necessary. I'll be fine."

He swiped a hand through his hair and headed toward the door. "If you're sure. . ."

"I'm sure."

"Good night, then." With one last worried glance, he exited the room.

Exhausted emotionally and physically, Cassidy sank down in the bed and fell asleep.

ॐ

Sunday morning dawned bright and sunny, promising a good day for the picnic. To Cassidy's disappointment, Dell was nowhere to be seen when they loaded up in the wagon and headed for town. She had dressed in the white cotton dress she'd worn on her wedding day. Somehow, she'd hoped he would see her and remember the tenderness they'd shared.

The schoolhouse was full when they arrived, so they found seats in the back. The service began with hymns. The sound of voices lifted in praise to God brought a thrill to Cassidy's soul. Although there were no instruments to accompany the voices, she had never heard a symphony which sounded more beautiful.

"Psst. . .psst. . .Cassidy!"

Several people turned around as Tarah gained her attention.

"What is it?" Cassidy whispered.

"I'm not feeling well. May I go to the wagon?"

Concerned, her gaze roved across the girl's face. More than likely she was just sleepy from reading so late, but Cassidy didn't want to take any chances. She nodded. "Do you want me to come with you?"

"Oh, no," the girl replied, quickly. "I just need to lie down for awhile."

They were causing a stir among the congregation, and even the minister was glancing their way.

"Go ahead, then," Cassidy whispered.

Conspicuously, Tarah stood and tiptoed to the door, causing every eye to turn. Once she was out the door, the preacher cleared his throat loudly to regain everyone's attention.

Cassidy sat through the rest of the sermon, soaking up the atmosphere. Although she was sorry to admit it, the message was somewhat lacking. The minister bounced from subject to subject—sin to sin. She supposed since he only got through the town once every few months, he wanted to hit on all the human vices possible to get the little congregation through until his next visit.

Cassidy fought the urge to squirm when he broached the subject of deception. She knew she was deceiving Dell by not telling him about the baby and that she would have to tell him soon. *I'm just so afraid of his reaction, Lord,* she prayed, knowing, even as the words lifted from her heart, that the excuse was not a good one. Part of honoring her husband required honesty. Repenting, she determined she would tell him that very day, no matter what the outcome.

Some of the older men were beginning to nod off, and even the most devout among the women were stirring uncomfortably on the hard wooden benches when the preacher finally dismissed the service.

Emily jumped from her seat and grabbed Cassidy's hand. "Ma, come and meet Miss Nelson."

She practically dragged Cassidy to the front of the building. "Miss Nelson, this is my ma," she announced proudly.

The young woman was indeed as lovely as Emily had

promised. Her chestnut hair was netted in a stylish chignon, and she looked out at Cassidy from clear blue eyes.

"Why, Mrs. St. John," she said in a low, smooth drawl, "how lovely to meet you."

"Likewise, Miss Nelson," Cassidy replied, feeling herself drawn by the depth of feeling in the woman's voice. "Emily has certainly been singing your praises all week."

The teacher glanced down fondly at the little girl. "Emily and I get along just fine, but. . ." A frown furrowed her lovely brow. "May I speak candidly?"

"Certainly, Miss Nelson."

"Please, call me Aimee," she said with a smile.

Cassidy returned her smile, feeling at ease. "All right. What would you like to talk to me about, Aimee?"

Aimee chewed her bottom lip and glanced cautiously at Emily. Taking the hint, Cassidy turned to the little girl. "Emily, Sweetheart, why don't you go to the wagon and tell everyone I'll be right there?"

"Aw, Ma," Emily replied, but she did as she was told.

Cassidy turned expectantly to the teacher, who gestured toward a bench. "Let's sit down," she suggested.

Once they were seated, Aimee drew a deep breath. "It's about Luke," she began.

Tension gnawed at Cassidy's insides as she waited for the teacher to continue.

"He is quite a handful and most disruptive, even destructive, in class."

Tension turned to alarm. "What sorts of things does he do?"

Aimee paused, then the words came spilling out. "He puts nails in the student's chairs, dips ribbons in ink wells, pulls the girls' hair, and just Friday he. . ." She shuddered. "He put a snake in my desk drawer! I almost fainted, Mrs. St. John. Can you imagine the chaos in my school if I had fainted in front of my class?"

Cassidy could well imagine.

"I might have lost my job."

Well, Cassidy doubted that, since there were no other teachers interested in coming to the rustic town for a teaching position that paid only twenty-five dollars for the three month term. Still, her heart went out to the young woman. Luke was difficult enough to deal with at home under his father's stern hand. In the classroom with only this young woman who was barely older than Tarah, she could imagine how unruly he could be.

She reached forward and placed a hand over Aimee's. "I'll have a talk with him."

Relief passed over the lovely features of the woman sitting beside her. "Thank you." She glanced down at her hands. "This is my first teaching position, and I didn't want the school board to feel I couldn't handle it myself. But standing in the corner is simply another way for Luke to disrupt and gain attention. I–I have never believed in corporal punishment, but a whipping may be what he needs."

Yes, a whipping might be exactly what he needed, unless. . . Cassidy held back the laughter bubbling up inside of her as an idea formed in her mind. She would teach the little monster a lesson. She stood and held out her hand to Aimee.

Aimee stood as well and accepted the proffered hand. "I don't want to cause any trouble, Mrs. St. John."

Mrs. St. John. Cassidy loved to be called that. Each time she heard the name a thrill moved up and down her spine.

"I assure you, you've caused no trouble for anyone who doesn't deserve it. I promise you, Luke will be dealt with, and if he isn't better on Monday, send a note home with one of the other children."

"All right," Aimee agreed, relief evident in her voice.

"I must be going, now. We have family plans. But it was very nice to meet you, and don't worry," she reassured the teacher. "You're doing a fine job with the rest of the children. Luke is just a difficult case."

Quick tears sprang to Aimee's eyes. "Thank you."

Cassidy smiled and squeezed her hand before saying her farewell. With a feeling of anticipation, she walked out of the church to the waiting wagon.

She frowned, looking around for Tarah.

"It's about time," Ellen huffed. "We've been sweltering out here."

It didn't seem that hot to Cassidy, but rather than comment, she asked, "Where is Tarah? I thought she came out here to lie down in the wagon."

"We thought she went back inside."

Oh, where was that girl? Cassidy's eyes scanned the little town, looking for the gingham dress Tarah had worn to church that morning.

"Everyone stay here so no one else gets lost," she commanded and left the wagon to begin her search. First she reentered the schoolhouse to be sure Tarah hadn't gone back inside. There was no sign of her. Next she walked outside and checked the privy. Still no Tarah.

Fear and frustration combined inside Cassidy's stomach, forming a large knot. She stopped and asked several of Tarah's friends if they'd seen her, but no one had. Cassidy once again scanned the little town for any sight of the lost girl. Suddenly her eyes focused on a familiar horse tethered outside the general store. It belonged to Johnny, the ranch foreman. Cassidy shuddered, remembering their encounter in the barn.

Now why would Johnny's horse be in town on Sunday? The general store wasn't even open.

Suspicion built inside of her, and she decided to investigate. She walked through the pathway between the store and the building next to it, around to the back. A gasp escaped her lips as she spied the familiar gingham-clad girl in Johnny's arms.

Anger welled up inside Cassidy, and she stormed toward the pair. Grabbing Tarah's arm, she jerked her away. "Johnny Cooper, you get your hands off my daughter, and don't ever let me catch you near her again. Do you hear me?"

"How dare you? You're not my mother." Tarah's eyes

sparked in fury.

"Be quiet and get to the wagon right now, young lady. We'll talk about this later."

Apparently too stunned to argue, Tarah emitted a strangled sob and ran down the alleyway toward the wagon.

Cassidy turned back to Johnny. "I mean it, Johnny. Don't you ever come near that child again."

Johnny stood in stunned silence as Cassidy whirled around and stormed to the wagon. Arms crossed, Tarah sat seething in the back of the wagon, tears of fury still pooling in her eyes. Without a word, Cassidy climbed into the seat and flapped the rcins, leading the horses toward the ranch.

First Luke and now Tarah. Give me wisdom, Lord!

ten

Cassidy's heart did a strange little flip-flop as she pulled hard on the reins, halting the wagon in front of the house. Dell sat on the porch awaiting their return.

Jumping from the wagon, Tarah flounced inside without a word.

Dell raised a questioning eyebrow at Cassidy.

Shaking her head, she shrugged. No sense ruining the day if she could help it. And telling Dell she had caught his daughter with the likes of Johnny Cooper would serve no purpose right now. A twinge of guilt made Cassidy hesitate, but she pushed it back. After all, she reasoned, if Dell found out, he would beat the living daylights out of Johnny and send him packing. And if he did that, Tarah would never get over the despicable man. No. The girl had to see Johnny for what he was and make the decision herself.

"You getting down from there today?"

Cassidy glanced down. Dell stood with a hand extended, ready to help her from the wagon.

"Sorry," she murmured, throwing him a sheepish grin.

"All right, everyone change out of your Sunday clothes and let's get going," Dell called, giving Cassidy support while she climbed down from the wagon.

"Everyone but you, that is. You keep that dress on." His voice was low, husky, and filled with longing. He'd noticed. Cassidy's heart went wild as his gaze caressed her. Was that love reflected in the blue depths of his eyes? Then why did he stay away? She pushed the disturbing thoughts aside for the moment and enjoyed walking to the house, hand in hand, with the man she loved.

Once inside, Dell left her to get the fishing poles while

123

Cassidy busied herself collecting the picnic fare.

"Want me to carry anything for you?"

Cassidy glanced up in surprise to find Sam, hands in his pockets, staring red faced at his boots. *Ah, he's making up!*

"Thanks, Sam. I'd appreciate it," she said, keeping her voice steady as she handed him the platter laden with fried chicken.

"Smells good," he said and walked carefully to the door, then turned to her.

"Thanks for not snitching Luke out to Pa last night. He'd a got a lickin' for sure."

"He probably deserves one," Cassidy said, giving him a wry smile in spite of herself. "Did he ever find the snake?"

"Nah, it's long gone." Sam shook his head. "We never thought you'd faint, though. Scared us half to death." With that, he left the house. Would wonders never cease?

Emily appeared at the kitchen door dressed in her everyday clothes, bonnet hanging by its strings around her neck. "Can Warrior come with us, Ma?"

Barefoot and wearing his new war bonnet as usual, Jack stood beside Emily. Each child stared at her with imploring eyes.

Tenderness for her youngest children welled up inside Cassidy, and she knew she could deny them nothing at this moment. "I don't see why not," she said with a smile. "He'd probably enjoy a day of splashing about in the creek."

Jack let out a war whoop and threw his arms around Cassidy. "You're the best ma ever!"

Tears stung her eyes as she watched the two children bound out the door, calling for the puppy.

Ellen limped into the kitchen next, and the two women made the final preparations for the picnic. After the wagon was loaded with family and food, Cassidy took a final peek around the kitchen and decided it was time to put her plans for Luke into action. She went to the spice cabinet and took down a small bag she had brought with her from Missouri.

Tucking it into her apron pocket, she set out to join her impatient family.

A grinning Dell stood beside the wagon when Cassidy stepped onto the porch.

Cassidy's heart leapt. He'd saddled Abby for her.

"Thought you might like to ride horseback today."

"Oh, yes, Dell. I would love it. Thank you." She grabbed the reins and lifted a foot into the stirrup.

"Cassidy," Ellen said cautiously.

"What?"

Ellen gave a pointed gaze at Cassidy's stomach.

Maybe horseback wasn't the best thing for the baby. "O–Oh right." She placed her foot back on the ground and turned to Dell. "Thanks anyway, but I think I'd rather ride in the wagon today."

With a small frown, he helped her up to the seat.

"I'll ride Abby, Pa." Tarah stood in the wagon and jumped down. "Since Cassidy doesn't want to."

"It's your ma's horse. You'll have to ask her."

Cassidy cringed at his reference to her as ma. She drew a breath, wondering what Tarah would say.

Eyes blazing, the girl turned to her. "May I?"

Exhaling in relief, Cassidy smiled. "Of course I don't mind. It will do her some good to be ridden."

"Thank you," Tarah replied through gritted teeth. Taking the reins from her father, she mounted and headed off toward the creek.

Dell glanced after her with a puzzled frown, then climbed onto his own horse. "Do you want to explain what just happened between the two of you?" he asked.

"Oh, a little disagreement," was all Cassidy said, and, thankfully, Dell dropped the matter.

"Let's go, then," he said, following Tarah's lead.

They found a secluded spot surrounded by shady trees and tall prairie grass. Enlisting the help of all the children and Dell, Cassidy had the picnic ready in no time. They sat around a red-and-white checkered tablecloth spread out on the ground. The tension seemed to fade away. Even Warrior had a feast of the chicken bones, and soon everyone was ready for dessert.

Cassidy cut the cake, serving Dell first, then Ellen, and continuing until everyone but Luke had a piece of the fluffy treat.

"Land sakes. I'm a plate short," Cassidy said, placing a hand to her cheek. "I know I counted right. Wait just a minute." She strolled to the wagon and grabbed the last plate. Glancing cautiously about to make sure no one watched, she gingerly pulled the little packet from her pocket. Sprinkling some of the red powder on the plate, she carefully walked back to the picnic spot. No one paid any attention to her as she cut the last piece of cake and placed it on Luke's plate. They were too engrossed in Dell's story of the Indian chief he'd seen in Abilene.

Luke took the plate from Cassidy's hands. "Hope this is edible." He threw Tarah a sideways glance, obviously trying to get a rise out of her.

Sticking out her tongue in retaliation, Tarah turned back to her pa's story.

Biting the inside of her cheeks to keep from laughing out loud, Cassidy waited while Luke wolfed down two large bites of the cake without stopping to taste it. Suddenly his eyes grew wide, and he grabbed the nearest glass of lemonade.

"Ah-wa-wa!" he cried, waving his hand over his mouth.

"Cut it out, Luke. We're trying to listen to Pa." Sam said, giving his brother a deep frown.

"Water, gimme water."

"Get your own."

"Luke St. John, you stop your foolishness, this minute," Ellen grumped.

"Hot! Hot!" Luke jumped up and ran for the creek.

Ellen shook her head while the rest of the family watched him in irritated silence.

"What that boy won't do for attention," Dell muttered. "I

better go have a talk with him."

Grabbing a corn muffin, Cassidy stood and glanced around the little group. "I'll see to him. Continue your story, Dell."

When she reached the boy, he was slapping handfuls of water on his tongue. He looked up with eyes smoldering in accusation. "You tried to poison me!"

"Don't be ridiculous," Cassidy replied calmly, dropping to the ground beside him. "Here, eat this. Water will only make it burn worse."

Grudgingly, he grabbed the muffin and devoured it, relaxing slowly as it took away the burn in his mouth.

"What'd you put in my cake?"

"That's my secret."

"Why'd you do that to me?" His eyes sparked with anger.

"It's no fun to be on the receiving end of a prank is it?" she asked quietly.

"I'll say."

"Now, I think you and I are even." She eyed him sternly. "But there's the little matter of Miss Nelson."

Caught, the boy swallowed hard and stared into the water.

"She tells me you're still creating problems in class. That true?"

"Well. . .I guess so."

"Hmm. Suppose we make a deal."

Luke eyed her suspiciously. "Like what?"

"I don't want to find anymore snakes, frogs, or bugs in my bed. No more rocks in my bath water. And I don't want to hear of you causing any problems in class. Is that understood?"

Red-faced, he nodded grudgingly.

"And for my part, I'll make sure your food is edible."

"Mas aren't supposed to put hot stuff in their kids' food, anyway," he informed her.

"Well, I've never been a ma before, and I'm sorry if I don't do it very well. But the threat of a thrashing didn't seem to keep you out of trouble, so I came up with my own solution. Now do we have a deal?" She held out a hand.

Cautiously he shook her hand and, to Cassidy's surprise, gave her a wide grin. "Aw, I guess you're all right." He stood. "I'd sure like to know what you put on my cake so I can do it to Sam sometime."

"Luke!" Cassidy declared firmly, fighting to keep from grinning back at him. "A deal is a deal. No more pranks!"

He looked at her in disbelief. "Not even on Sam and the rest of the kids?"

"Well, just don't hurt anyone, destroy any property, or do it at school."

"Yes, Ma'am," he said and ran back to the little party around the picnic blanket.

A chuckle escaped her lips. Well, a tiger couldn't change his stripes, but he could be tamed, so they said. Fun and games were part of what made Luke who he was, and as long as he didn't get out of hand, she could grant him a little freedom.

What a day this was turning out to be! Cassidy sighed with contentment and stretched her legs out in front of her. She leaned back on her arms, watching the sun shining down on the rippling creek. Suddenly, she felt a flutter inside. She placed a hand on her stomach and felt the flutter again. Her baby was moving! Tears formed in her eyes and streamed down her cheeks.

"Everything all right?" Dell dropped down beside her.

"Yes," Cassidy replied, quickly wiping her tears away with the back of her hand.

"Then why are you crying?" he insisted softly.

"I'm just happy. I have a home and children and this has been such a wonderful day. I guess I just became over-whelmed with God's goodness." She smile at him, then threw a glance back to where Ellen was clearing away the food. "I'd better go help."

Dell placed a restraining hand on her arm as she started to get up.

"Mother gave me strict instructions that you are not to move from this spot until she and Tarah finish cleaning up."

Cassidy shrugged. It felt so good to relax that she wasn't going to argue the point.

A loud splash caught their attention. Glancing toward the laughing children, Cassidy watched the playful antics of Jack and Emily in the water. Warrior jumped in behind them, barking wildly.

Dell stretched out on the grassy bank, using his arm behind his head for a pillow.

Another flutter from the baby sent a tremor of happiness through Cassidy, and she longed to tell her husband of the child's existence. Swallowing hard, she glanced down at him. "Dell?"

"Hmm?" He opened one eye and stared up at her.

Suddenly, Emily screamed. "Jack, come back!"

Cassidy shot to her feet and ran into the water. Jack was caught in a current pushing him downstream.

A scream tore at her throat, and without thought, she dove into the water and swam for all she was worth. "Hang on, Jack. Hang on."

"Ma! Help me!"

The current was rough, and she felt it dragging at her long dress. She kicked hard against the weight. Finally she reached the little boy, but Dell was already there. He grabbed Jack around the waist just as the little boy was pulled under. Jack flailed his arms wildly.

"I have you," Dell reassured. "Be still and don't struggle."

Gulping in a large mouthful of water, Cassidy coughed frantically. Seeing that Jack was safely in his father's arms, she swam as hard as she could toward the nearest bank. Dragging her aching body from the river, she collapsed onto the grass. Dell was right behind her, carrying Jack. Cassidy sat up and held out her arms for the child. Pulling her son onto her lap, she wrapped her arms about him as tight as she could without hurting him.

"Are you all right, sweet boy?" she asked, tears streaming down her face.

"Yeah, Ma." Jack was already recovered from the ordeal and began to wiggle in her arms.

Cassidy kissed him hard, then let him go. He ran back to meet up with the other children, who hurried along the bank toward him. The way he recounted his ordeal with such enthusiasm, one would have thought it was a grand adventure.

Exhausted, Cassidy lay back on the ground. Closing her eyes, she sent up a prayer of thanks.

Suddenly a shadow fell across her. She opened her eyes to find Dell standing over her, his gaze resting on her stomach. Glancing down, she saw the white cotton dress molded to her body, revealing the small mound where their child grew inside her. The look of horror on his face said it all, and she placed a protective hand across the growing infant.

His gaze traveled from her stomach, up her body, to her eyes. "Are you all right?" he asked.

With a fatigued wave of her hand, Cassidy nodded.

"Are you pregnant?" His tone was guarded and clipped.

"Yes." She met his gaze defiantly. After all there was no shame in carrying her husband's baby, even if he didn't want her or the child.

"Is this why Mother insisted you get more rest—she knows?"

A short laugh left her lips. "Ellen's the one who told me."

"Why did you keep it from me?"

Cassidy thought she detected hurt in his voice, but when she looked into his eyes, they glittered hard. Disappointment clouded her heart. "Why indeed?" she replied bitterly. "You've been so sweet and tender lately, I don't know why I didn't tell you immediately."

His eyes narrowed at her sarcasm, but Cassidy was undaunted by the warning flash and continued. "Maybe I just wanted to enjoy my happiness for awhile before you spoiled it for me!"

She sat up and a wave of nausea overtook her. Turning her head, she lost her lunch on the bank of the creek. Silently, Dell took her into his arms while tears of humiliation fell from her eyes.

"Shh," he crooned. "Don't cry, my darling, the sickness doesn't last very long."

Suddenly, Cassidy exploded in frustration. "You ignoramus," she said, jerking back from his arms. "Do you really think I'm crying because I'm sick?"

Dell blinked in surprise and sat dumbfounded as she vented.

"I am thirty-five years old and have never borne a child. I welcome the sickness. I glory in it! I thank God every day knowing there is a life within me."

"Calm down," Dell said softly, gathering her back in his arms.

More frustrated than ever, Cassidy pushed him away from her. "You are a stubborn, stupid man and I don't know why I fell in love with you." Rising to her feet, she clamped her hands down hard on her hips. "We had two wonderful days and nights together and could have had a lifetime of happiness, but you decided to push me away. Well, be mad all you want about this baby. I'm happy. Ecstatic, in fact, and I will be for the rest of my life. So there!"

Cassidy stomped back to the picnic area before he could say a word. Trembling, she leaned against the wagon and cried. Minutes later, when the tears were spent, she gave a determined lift to her chin, a decision made. She would not cry again! There were too many blessings to count for her to moon about and pine for a man who clearly only wanted her as a mother for his children—his older children, that is. It was time for her to settle in and enjoy motherhood. God was so good. And she would enjoy this pregnancy if it was the last thing she ever did! Dell or no Dell.

≈

Dell lay tormented on his bed that night. He wanted to go to Cassidy, to hold her and reassure her of his love, but something held him back. Once again he bargained with God.

"You took Anna from me when I broke my promise. But

I'll keep my end of the bargain this time, God. Let Cassidy live, and I won't touch her again while she's still young enough to have children."

In his mind, the years loomed ahead of him, and unbidden came the words Reverend Marcus had spoken the night Dell had attended the service on the trail. "God doesn't bargain with man. His ways are too high for that."

Dell squirmed on the tick mattress. Well, the preacher was wrong. God did bargain with man. He bargained, and man paid dearly if he didn't keep his end of the deal. Del had loved Anna, but his own lack of control had killed her. That would not happen with Cassidy. She was like a fresh spring breeze blowing through this dry dusty land, and he refused to lose her.

When she jumped in the water after Jack, he had thought his heart would pound from his chest as fear rose up inside of him. A knot formed in his stomach at the thought of what might have happened to Jack and Cassidy. And to find out she was going to have a baby nearly did him in!

He'd watched Cassidy carefully the rest of the afternoon and insisted she go to bed as soon as she got home. She'd balked at the pampering, but gave in when Ellen agreed with Dell.

"Oh, fine. I'll go lie down, but it really isn't necessary."

When he looked in on her fifteen minutes later, she'd been sound asleep, a peaceful smile resting on her lips.

Dell emitted a low chuckle at the memory. How he loved that woman. But God was testing him, and her life was the prize, just like with Anna. The difference was that this time, he wouldn't fail.

❧

Storm clouds invaded the skies the following morning as Cassidy loaded the breakfast table with fluffy hot cakes and sizzling bacon. She looked on with loving amusement while the children and Dell devoured the sumptuous fare as though they hadn't eaten in a month. A rumble of thunder sounded in the distance, and Dell pushed back from his plate.

"Better get a move on before the storm comes," he instructed the children. "I'll take you to school this morning." He reached forward and tousled Jack's unruly curls. "Want to ride along, Son?" The little boy's head bobbed as he shoved in one last bite of breakfast. Dell headed outside to hook up the team while the older children grabbed their books.

Cassidy stood at the open door with lunches in hand, ready to pass them out as the children bounded toward the wagon. Jack and Emily each kissed Cassidy before running outside with shouts of, " 'Bye, Ma!" Luke grabbed his lunch and started to head out the door.

"Wait, Luke. Remember our deal."

Throwing her a wide grin, he nodded and ran for the wagon.

Sam grabbed his lunch and paused, then reached over and gave her a peck on the cheek. "Bye, Ma," he said softly. Speechless, she watched him go. With her heart still full of wonder, she faced Tarah's glittering eyes.

"Don't expect me to call you 'ma.' "

Deflated, Cassidy turned back to the table and sat to finish her coffee. "I don't expect any of you to, but I'm happy the boys are beginning to accept me."

"Tarah, let's go," Dell shouted from the wagon.

"You said I wouldn't have to go after the first week." Tarah's eyes sparked with challenge.

With a sigh, Cassidy went back to the door. "Go on without her. Tarah's staying home today."

"She okay?"

"She's fine. Just go before the rain starts."

With a wave, Dell flicked the reins and the wagon lurched forward.

Cassidy stepped back to the table and began filling a breakfast plate for Ellen, who was in her bed after the excitement of the day before. "If you're staying home, you can help me."

Tarah opened her mouth to protest, but Cassidy raised a hand. "No arguments. Take this plate to your granny. She's feeling poorly."

"Fine."

"And then come back and help me clean up." Cassidy ignored the anger flashing in the violet eyes and busied herself washing the dishes.

Tarah flounced away. When she returned a few moments later, she grabbed a towel to dry the dishes.

"You had no right to drag me away from Johnny like that," Tarah began. "We were doing nothing wrong."

"You don't consider lying to get out of church, then kissing a man twice your age to be wrong?"

"Well. . .the lying part was wrong, but there was no other way to see him alone."

"You shouldn't be seeing him at all. Let alone kissing him."

Cassidy searched frantically to find the words that would reach the girl.

"Johnny and I love each other," Tarah insisted. "We are going to be married."

A knot formed in Cassidy's stomach. "Tarah, you haven't. . ."

The girl blushed to the roots of her hair, and her eyes grew wide. "Of course not," she gasped. "What kind of a woman do you think I am?"

Relieved, Cassidy gave her a wry smile. "To be honest, I don't think of you as a woman. You're still so young."

Tarah lifted her chin.

"But," Cassidy continued, "I can see that you are close to womanhood, and I wouldn't want you to get hooked up with the wrong man."

"Johnny is not the wrong man!"

"I thought there was another boy you were interested in— Anthony something or other."

Tarah tossed her head. "Anthony Greene. I wouldn't give that child the time of day. Besides, he's smitten with Louisa Thomas."

"I see. . ."

"Are you going to tell Pa about Johnny?"

"I don't know, Tarah. I think he should know."

"But he'll fire Johnny if he finds out."

If Johnny's lucky, he'll get off with just being fired, Cassidy thought. Looking at Tarah, she said, "I can't worry about that. Unless. . ."

Hope rose in Tarah's ashen face but left quickly at Cassidy's words.

"Unless you promise me you won't have anything more to do with the likes of Johnny Cooper."

"You can't ask me to do that. I love him!"

"Then you leave me no choice but to speak to your father."

A sob escaped Tarah's throat, and she threw the towel on the counter. "All right. I won't see him anymore. I can't have him lose his job because of me."

She ran out the door, tears streaming down her lovely face.

Cassidy picked up the towel and finished wiping the dishes, praying for Tarah as she did so. "Mend her heart, Father. Young love is the cruelest love of all."

eleven

Cassidy lay snuggled under her thick quilt listening to the wind howl outside. She glanced out of the window as a bolt of lightning connected heaven to earth in one long, jagged streak. Immediately, a crash of thunder followed, shaking the house to its foundation. She shivered at the violence of the storm. "Lord," she prayed. "Keep us all safe in Your arms while the tempest rages around us."

As if responding to her voice, the baby gave a hard kick. Cassidy smiled and placed a loving hand over her stomach. "Sorry to wake you, little one, but your ma can't sleep with all the racket outside." The baby rolled inside of her, causing Cassidy to giggle with the wonder of creation.

Suddenly, her door flew open and Dell stood, clad in Levis, his flannel shirt open to the waist. "Get up." His gaze rested on her for only a second before he continued down the hall.

Throwing off the covers, she jumped and ran into the hallway as Dell pounded on each door. "Everyone out of bed, quickly," he called.

"Dell? What's wrong?"

"The storm is bad. Could be a twister, and I don't want to take any chances. Get your bedding," he ordered. "We're going to the root cellar."

"A twister in the middle of November?"

"When the temperature drops as quickly as it did this afternoon, there are always bad storms. Now hurry!"

Cassidy flew into action as the children gathered around, rubbing sleepy eyes.

"Get a blanket," Dell commanded them, "and come with me."

"What is going on here?" Ellen appeared at her door, clad in her dressing gown.

"We're going to the cellar," Cassidy explained. "Dell's afraid the storm will turn into a twister."

"Hogwash. I'm going back to bed."

As she turned to go, Jack let up a howl. "No, Granny. Come with us. I don't want you to get blown away!"

He threw his arms tightly about her, and she glanced helplessly at the little boy.

"Oh, all right," she relented. "Now stop crying."

Dell grabbed up little Jack and headed for the front door. He began opening it carefully, but the ferocious wind snatched the wooden door away from him, slamming it hard against the outside wall.

"Ma!" Emily screamed in terror, burying her head into Cassidy's bulging middle.

"Shh, it's all right."

She held the little girl tightly as they lowered their heads and struggled against the wind.

"Hang onto the rail," Dell shouted.

The root cellar was between the house and the soddy, and they reached it quickly.

Cassidy waited while Dell helped each child inside, then Ellen.

She took a step toward Dell's outstretched arm, but stopped as Warrior barked from across the yard.

"Come on, Boy," she called.

Suddenly, she heard a yelp as a slat blew off the barn roof and hit the animal, knocking him down.

"Warrior!" screamed Emily.

He lay motionless where he'd fallen.

"Come on!" yelled Dell.

Without stopping to think, Cassidy took off across the yard, fighting the wind. Relieved to find the animal still breathing, she bent and gathered him in her arms. He whimpered as she jostled him. "Come on, Boy. I have you." She glanced fearfully at the barn as its door blew open. Abby broke out of her stall and ran out, bucking and neighing wildly around the fenced barnyard.

A flash of lightning brightened the sky, and for a moment Cassidy saw the twister extending from the heavens. Frozen, she could only watch as the funnel swirled toward her, tearing up everything in its path.

Suddenly, she felt Dell grab her and half-carry, half-drag her back to the cellar, then pull her inside.

"Are you crazy?" he barked. "Your life and the life of my child is more important than a dog's."

"I–I'm sorry, Dell. I guess I just wasn't thinking straight. I saw him lying there, hurt, and I just reacted. Besides, h–he's not just a dog, he's part of the family."

"Thunder and lightning," he muttered.

He grabbed the door and started to pull it down, when Johnny appeared, shaking in fear. "It's a twister!"

"We know. Get in and close the door," Dell said gruffly. Turning, he ordered, "Give me the dog, Cassidy."

Cassidy did as she was told. Dell laid the animal gently on the floor and looked him over. A gash on Warrior's side seeped blood, but the wound wasn't fatal. Dell removed his shirt and wrapped it tightly around the animal to stop the bleeding.

Tarah held Emily protectively against her side but looked out shyly from beneath long lashes at Johnny as he walked to the back wall and sank down.

He threw a cautious glance at Dell, then winked at the girl.

Cassidy bristled and cleared her throat. Receiving the full impact of her stern glare, Tarah shifted her gaze to the dirt floor. Giving Johnny what she hoped was a look of intimidation, Cassidy was rewarded with a very unintimidated, insolent grin.

Tarah had been true to her word the past two months, steering clear of the ranch hand, and had even returned to school. Cassidy's heart sank to realize the girl was still infatuated with Johnny. Perhaps she'd have to speak to Dell after all. She looked toward her husband. His worried gaze was riveted on the closed door above them. In an act of boldness, she went to him and slipped her hand in his. He gripped it hard and turned to her. Tears glistened in his eyes, and Cassidy rested her cheek against his bare arm. "It'll be all right, Dell. God will take care of us."

"Come on," he said quietly. "You need to sit."

He led her back to her space against the wall and sat beside her. Grabbing the quilt, he draped it over her.

Cassidy lifted the edge closest to Dell and pulled it over him. "You'll be sick with no shirt on," she admonished. "Share the covers with me."

His gaze melted into hers, and he lifted his arm, wrapping it around her. The heat from his fingers against her upper arm sent a tremor through her middle.

When the baby kicked again, Cassidy smiled and grabbed Dell's other hand. He glanced down with hesitation in his eyes as she placed his hand on her stomach. The baby greeted his father with a strong kick. Dell pulled his hand away, as though he'd touched a hot stove, then placed it gingerly back on the mound. He laid his head against Cassidy's while he became acquainted with his unborn child.

Overwhelming contentment washed over Cassidy, and she snuggled against Dell, enjoying the closeness even while the storm raged over them. *Peace in the midst of the storm, Lord. This is what You've given me.*

They sat huddled together on the dirt floor, wrapped in thick quilts, while the storm spent its rage above them. For a time, they could hear nothing but the roar of the wind and the banging of their belongings flying through the air. Suddenly everything died down, the twister leaving as quickly as it had come, though thunder rumbled and lightning still filtered in through the cracks in the wooden door.

"We'll stay here for awhile to be certain," Dell informed them. "Storms like this can go on all night."

He was right. Though there were no more twisters, the wind rose and died down several times, and the storm blew until just before dawn.

When morning came, every inch of Cassidy's body ached from her night spent on the hard ground. She dreaded what they would find when they looked outside.

Getting up from beside her, Dell climbed the cellar steps. Drawing a slow breath, he lifted the latch and threw the door open. A blast of cold air blew into the cellar, and white flakes filtered in.

"Is it snowing?" Cassidy asked incredulously.

Dell nodded.

From the back of the room, Johnny groaned. "That's going to make it a bear to get things cleaned up."

Cassidy sent him a scathing glance, then shifted her attention back to Dell.

"How bad is it?" she asked.

"Barn's gone, but the house is fine."

Relief filled her at the news. *Thank You, Lord, for sparing our home.*

One by one, they emerged from the cellar. Dell's shoulders slumped as he stared at the wreckage caused by the storm, and Cassidy's heart ached for him. Chickens lay dead, strewn across the yard. Splintered boards lay on the ground where the tall barn had stood just hours earlier. Tree limbs and slats decorated the area. Cassidy's lips quivered at the extent of the devastation, and she struggled for composure. At least they could thank God that they were all safe and that the house had been spared.

"Darling," Dell said quietly, taking her by the shoulders and steering her toward the house. "I want you to go inside and get into bed."

"But I have to get breakfast," she protested.

Dell's gaze shifted to Tarah.

"I'll help Granny fix breakfast," she offered. "You should lie down like Pa says."

With a sigh, Cassidy nodded. She stepped over fallen limbs and other clutter in the yard and on the porch. Once inside the house, she looked around. A few knickknacks and pictures had fallen, but all in all, everything looked pretty much the way they had left it the night before.

Cassidy made her way back to her bedroom, opened her bureau drawer, and lifted out a fresh nightgown. Changing quickly, she climbed into bed, pulling the covers over her shivering body. It didn't matter that the edges of the quilt were dirty from the cellar floor. She'd wash it later. For now, she was too tired to care.

With a yawn and another prayer of thanks, Cassidy drifted to sleep, smiling at the memories from the night—of Dell's hand covering her stomach, his arm wrapped tightly about her shoulders. The last thing she remembered before sleep claimed her was that he had called her "darling" in the light of day.

❧

A light dusting of snow fell from the sky as Dell surveyed the damage to the barn. Even with five ranch hands working alongside him, it would take awhile to get everything cleared away and begin rebuilding.

Luckily, the horses had emerged from the storm unscathed. For now, they and the milk cow would have to be put back into the old sod barn.

Dell sighed, surveying the work ahead of him. Yesterday, he and the hands had rounded up all the cattle they could find. Several had been lost, as well as a few pigs. He'd have to make another trip to Abilene to sell off some more of the stock if they were to make it through the winter. He hated to think of leaving Cassidy alone this far into her pregnancy, but it couldn't be helped.

The snow began to fall faster, and he cast a cursory glance toward the sky. Thick clouds blanketed the heavens, and a knot formed in his stomach. Winter had arrived in earnest after the storm, and those clouds indicated more snow was coming. Spurred into action at the thought, he stepped forward, lifting a splintered board from the pile of rubble. He knew he'd better get to work if the barn was to be rebuilt before the new year.

≈

Cassidy opened her eyes, then sat up quickly as her ears registered more howling wind.

Not another storm. Oh, God, please, no.

She pushed the covers and sat up, shivering. She swung her feet down to the floor, and lifted them up just as quickly. The floor was icy. And yesterday had started out as warm as a day in July! Gingerly she stepped down onto the cold floor, slipped into her house shoes, and walked to the window. A thin layer of frost covered the glass, making it impossible to see outside. With the edge of her nightgown, she made a circle in the glistening white ice. She peeked through the opening but could see nothing in the darkness.

Frustrated, she grabbed her dressing gown and slipped it on. "I'll go look out the front door," she muttered. She lifted her shawl from its peg and threw it around her shoulders.

When she reached the sitting room, she stopped. Dell stood by the front window, staring outside.

She moved forward until she stood beside him. "What is it?" she asked, fearful of the answer.

He laughed shortly. "Welcome to Kansas. First you witnessed a twister, now you get to experience a prairie blizzard."

Relief that it wasn't another twister was mixed with the dread of the snowstorm. She'd never seen a blizzard before, and watching the angry driving snow sent a shiver through her. Cassidy felt Dell shift, and her heart leaped as his arms captured her from behind.

Resting his hands on her stomach, he pressed her against him. The baby protested the heavy hands spread over Cassidy's stomach.

"This is going to be one strong boy," Dell said with a chuckle.

"Boy? I think not."

"Oh? And what's wrong with having a boy?"

"There are enough men in this family as it is," Cassidy said with a quick lift of her chin. "We need a girl to even things out."

"All right. A girl then," he said. "One who looks exactly like you."

"Oh, no! She mustn't look like me." Years of being over-looked at parties flashed through Cassidy's mind. "I want my daughter to be invited to dances and box socials. I want gen-tlemen to ask to escort her home when she's a young lady. She has to look like you," she finished firmly.

"Haven't you ever been asked to a dance?"

"Not one single time." In his arms, the sting was gone. Still she remembered the hurt of her younger years.

"Well, Mrs. St. John. I am formally asking you to allow me the honor of escorting you to the Christmas dance next month."

A giggle escaped her lips. "Mr. St. John, I accept."

With a sigh, she leaned her head back against his broad chest and covered his hands with her own. They stood in silence, for a time, Dell's chin resting on her head.

"Cassidy," he said quietly.

"Hmm?"

"I'm glad you decided to come with me."

Her pulse quickened, and she stroked the back of his hand. "Me, too."

He placed a gentle kiss on the top of her head, sending a shiver up her spine. "I love you," he whispered.

"You do?" It was the first time he'd ever said those words.

She felt him nod against her cheek.

"Yes, I reckon I do."

Tears formed in Cassidy's eyes.

"I know it doesn't seem that way, and you don't under-stand the arrangement we have, but my feelings for you are genuine."

He turned her around to face him in the eerie glow of the fire. "You've been a wonderful mother to my children, and somehow you've even gotten Mother to soften. You amaze me."

"Well, to be honest," Cassidy said, throwing him a saucy grin, "you were the one who got Ellen to soften."

A lifted brow was his response.

"It's true. She started being nice to me after she found out that I—well—about the baby."

At the reminder, Dell shifted. Taking her by the hand, he led her to a chair by the fireplace. "Come and sit," he said.

Grabbing a nearby stool, he brought it closer to the warmth of the fire and sat facing her. "We haven't really had the chance to discuss your condition," he said. "How are you getting along?"

"I'm feeling a little more uncomfortable as time goes by," she admitted. "But not enough to cause concern."

"You sure?" his eyes scrutinized her. "Don't do more than you should. There's no need to hurt yourself when Mother and Tarah can do for you."

Waving away his concern, Cassidy nevertheless felt a thrill that he cared enough to worry. "But there's no need for them do so many of the household duties. Ellen is feeble, and Tarah has her studies to attend to."

The look on Dell's face was firm. "I figure you have about three more months to go. That right?"

Cassidy felt her cheeks grow hot, but she held his gaze. "Two and a half."

"All right, then. For the next two and a half months, and for a few weeks after the baby is born, I expect you to take it easy. No heavy lifting, no more scrubbing over the clothes—"

"Oh, Dell, really," she interjected.

"Tarah is plenty old enough to take care of the washing on Saturdays," he insisted. "It's high time that girl learns to take care of a home, anyway."

"That may be, but I can't sit around all day with nothing to do while others tend to the chores I should be doing."

His eyes studied her for a moment, taking in face and body. He drew a breath, then exhaled slowly as he spoke. "You aren't like Anna."

Cassidy's heart sank as his gaze drifted from her up to the daguerreotype on the mantle. She knew he couldn't see the woman's image in the fire-lit room, but he stared as though he did.

"She was small and dainty. Frail, really. She was in bed almost from the beginning with Tarah. Weak and ill constantly. And it was worse with each child. I should never have. . ." He stood and walked to the window, glancing out into the predawn haze.

A glimmer of understanding dawned on Cassidy. "It wasn't your fault she died. Whatever caused you to think it was?"

A short, mirthless laugh escaped his lips. "When the time came for Luke to be born, she had a rough time of it. I promised myself and God that if she lived, I'd make sure she never got in that condition again—a promise I obviously didn't keep."

"Do you mean to tell me you think God took Anna because she was with child again?" The very thought was ludicrous, insulting to God, really. "He wouldn't do that."

"Well, He did." Dell's reply was clipped and filled with bitterness.

Somehow, she had to make him see. "God is merciful. He doesn't let people die out of revenge."

" 'Vengeance is mine; I will repay, saith the Lord.' " He threw her a wry smile. "You see, I know some Scripture."

"Don't joke about this, Dell. That verse does not mean God kills for revenge. That's the way of imperfect man, not a perfect, loving God."

"Then why did she die?" he asked, his eyes beseeching her for an answer.

"You said it yourself. She was frail—weakened a little more with each child."

"And I should have known better. Should have used more control."

Cassidy eased forward in the chair and lumbered to her feet. She went to Dell, wrapping her arms around him from behind. He tensed, but Cassidy pressed in.

"Women know what they want," she said softly, laying her

cheek against his back. "If Anna didn't want to have babies, she wouldn't have. Please don't blame yourself anymore."

Dell took a ragged breath and turned in her arms.

The tenderness reflected in his eyes melted Cassidy's heart and caused her to reach out. "I know I'm not Anna," she said, eyes filling with tears, "but I love you, Dell. And you say you love me. Can't we just put the past behind us and be happy?"

He cupped her face between his large hands. "I do love you, more than I ever thought possible."

Joy welled up inside Cassidy. "Oh, Dell."

"I'll be a good husband to you and a good father to our baby, but I won't take a chance on losing you, too."

"You won't lose me!"

"No more babies, Cass. I mean it. And the only way I can assure myself of that is to stay in the lean-to."

"Don't I have anything to say about it?"

"No," he said firmly. "Don't fight me on this. Please."

"All right," she relented. "I won't say any more to you about it." But that didn't mean she didn't intend to discuss the subject with God!

twelve

Dell released a sigh of relief as he left the town of Abilene behind. He hoped the ride home would be quicker than the trip to town had been. Countless troubles had assaulted him and Johnny while they tried to herd ten head of cattle through the deep snow. Now that the stock was sold, the runners on the bottom of the sled should take them home in no time.

He glanced over his shoulder at the supplies loaded in the sled and patted the saddlebags next to him on the seat. Relief filled him that the sale had brought in enough to carry them through the winter and a little beyond. He'd even had enough to buy Christmas gifts for his family and material for Cassidy to make garments for the baby.

His pulse quickened at the thought of the new child. It wouldn't be long now. Just a few more weeks. A sense of dread clenched his gut as he thought ahead. Would he still have Cassidy when it was all over or, like little Jack, would the new baby be left motherless?

Cassidy had waved away all of his concerns, and even Ellen had tried to reassure him that Cassidy was the type of woman who bore children easily. Still, Dell knew from experience that God could be ruthless in His dealings when men broke their word. And he was determined not to break his word this time.

He had found himself praying more lately. For the baby and Cassidy. For the other children, who thankfully were beginning to accept Cassidy into their lives—all but Tarah. Most of all, he prayed for strength to keep his promise to God. In unguarded moments, he wondered if perhaps Reverend Marcus had been right when he said life had just dealt him a harsh blow. That Anna's death had nothing to do with a bargain. And then Cassidy didn't believe that God was a God of vengeance, either.

Looking out at the glistening snow, Dell knew he was afraid to agree with her. Afraid to give in and be the husband Cassidy deserved, in every sense of the word. In spite of his resolve, somewhere deep inside, hope was beginning to glimmer.

≈

Cassidy caught her breath as the sleigh glided over the icy ground. The moon, full and bright, cast a silvery glow on the snow-covered plain. Oh, what a perfect evening it would have been if only Dell were there to share it. She sighed aloud, her breath frosty white in the frigid night air.

The first trip Dell made to Abilene only kept him away for two weeks. But this time he and Johnny had already been gone five weeks, and Cassidy was beginning to worry about her husband.

She glanced sideways at Sam and her heart swelled with pride—mother's pride. He sat with the reins in his capable hands, looking confident, almost manly, as he drove the horses.

Turning, he blushed bright red as he caught her staring at him.

She placed a gentle, gloved hand on his arm. "I was just thinking of what a big help you've been since your pa's been gone." He swallowed hard as she continued. "I truly don't know what I would have done without you."

"I only wish Pa woulda made it back for the dance tonight," he said softly. "I know how you've been looking forward to it."

"I am disappointed," she admitted. "But it couldn't be helped, and there will be other dances your pa can escort me to."

He nodded and turned his attention back to the horses.

Cassidy smiled, remembering the morning Dell had asked her to the Christmas dance. A small ache crossed her heart, making it feel as though it were bruised. She had hoped against hope that he would be back in time to escort her, but here she was again, going alone to a dance. Well, she wasn't really alone, she reminded herself. After all, the children were with her.

A slight twinge pinched her lower back. Mercy, this seat was uncomfortable! Thankfully they were pulling into town. She'd be glad to get out and stretch her legs.

Sam pulled the horses to a stop in front of the little school-house, maneuvering carefully around the other sleighs in the yard.

"Luke, help the girls," he ordered, jumping down. "I'll get Ma."

Sam walked around to her side, almost losing his footing on the icy ground. He lifted the heavy quilt from her lap. "Be careful," he admonished. "It's pretty slippery here."

She took his proffered hand, stepping down carefully. The rest of the children moved ahead of her, unmindful of the ice; but Sam stayed by Cassidy's side. He didn't release her until they were inside the building. Then he helped her out of her coat and led her carefully to a chair.

She patted his arm. "Thank you, Sam. Now go ask someone to dance."

A bright red glow covered his face and spread all the way to his hairline. He glanced around until his eyes rested on Camilla Simpson.

Ah, so he still had a crush on the girl.

Camilla's gaze shifted from the young man who whirled her around the dance floor, to Sam, and a pretty blush appeared on her cheeks.

From the looks of it, the feeling was mutual. Well, Cassidy didn't blame Camilla for having a crush on Sam. She only hoped the perky brunette was worthy of her special son.

"Go ahead and ask her to dance," she urged.

"Naw." Sam stuffed his hands into his trouser pockets. "I can't cut in on another fella."

With a sniff, Cassidy waved a hand. "Looks to me like she'd rather dance with you."

Indeed, Camilla seemed hard pressed to focus on the young man with whom she was dancing, for her eyes kept roving to Sam.

"Think so?"

"Seems pretty obvious," she said with a wry smile. "It's perfectly all right for a man to cut in on a dance. Just go tap her partner politely on the shoulder. If he's a gentleman, he'll move aside."

A look of indecision crossed his features.

"Go ahead." Cassidy gave him a small shove.

With his hands still stuffed in his pockets, he cleared his throat and took a tentative step onto the dance floor.

An encouraging smile touched Cassidy's lips as he glanced back at her. She inclined her head to spur him on. His back straightened, and he tapped Camilla's partner on the shoulder. He received a scowl from the lad, but a shy smile lit Camilla's face.

At the demonstration of new courtship, Cassidy's heart ached with loneliness. Deep in thoughts of Dell, she jumped when a man's voice broke into her thoughts. "It looks like we may end up in-laws."

With an upward glance, Cassidy recognized Camilla's father. She smiled. "Well, I wouldn't count my chickens before they're hatched," she replied. "But you could be right. Sam's pretty smitten."

"He's not the only one." A baritone chuckle escaped the doctor's lips. "Cammie's been miserable for weeks, wondering if your boy would ask her to dance tonight."

"Well, she needn't have worried."

Dr. Simpson took the chair next to her. "Uh, Mrs. St. John, I don't want to appear rude, but I can't help noticing your condition."

Heat warmed Cassidy's face and a gasp escaped her lips at the man's audacity.

He raised a hand in defense. "Pardon my boldness, but I am a doctor."

"Of course." Cassidy smiled.

"I'd like to offer my assistance when your time comes."

"That's generous of you, but I'm fine, really. I have a

woman at home to help me." She shifted in her seat as another twinge pinched her back. Would she ever be comfortable again?

"I realize you've had several children, Mrs. St. John, but you look as though you might deliver at any moment," he persisted. "It wouldn't hurt to have a doctor present at the birth."

"This is my first child, Doctor. And anyway, I have five or six weeks to go."

He frowned, and his gaze shifted to Sam and Camilla.

"My husband had four children before we met," Cassidy explained. "And I took my niece to raise after her parents died."

"And you said you still have a month to go?"

She nodded. "A little over a month."

"Hmm." His gaze roved over her bulging stomach. "You're a large built woman, so maybe you're just carrying a big baby."

Cassidy winced at the reference to her size. A big baby! She didn't want her girl to be big.

"At any rate," he said. "It might be a good idea to enlist my services when the time comes."

"I'll discuss it with my husband, Dr. Simpson. Thank you for your concern."

The song ended and the dancers drifted from the floor. Sam and Camilla made their way toward Cassidy.

Sam stretched out a hand to Camilla's father. "How are you tonight, Sir?"

The doctor grasped the proffered hand and gave Sam a good-natured grin. "Doing fine, Son." He glanced at Camilla. "How'd you like to dance with your pa?"

Camilla dimpled. "I'd love to."

Sam stuffed his hands into his pockets and cleared his throat. "You don't feel like dancing, do you?" he asked, his gaze resting on Cassidy.

Though she felt she probably shouldn't make a spectacle of herself in her condition, she couldn't resist. "I would be delighted."

"Uh, okay."

The hesitancy in his voice caused Cassidy's brows to furrow. "You sure you don't mind, Sam?"

His face colored.

So he was embarrassed to dance with her in her condition. "It's all right," she said, her heart going out to him. "We don't have to."

"No, it's okay. It would be my, uh, honor," he insisted, though Cassidy didn't quite believe him.

The grin that crossed his features, was the same heart-stopping smile she'd seen so many times on his father. Another ache crossed Cassidy's heart as he helped her to her feet.

She danced with her son until he stopped, abruptly. She glanced up into his face, but his pleased gaze rested beyond her. Cassidy turned. Dell! He stood at the door, watching her, and when he caught her gaze, his face lit up into a smile.

Tears of relief filled her eyes and she moved toward him as fast as her feet would take her.

Gathering her into his arms, Dell placed a light kiss on her lips.

"Dell," she admonished, "people are watching."

He shrugged and grinned. "If a man didn't kiss his wife after not seeing her for a month, I'd think there was something wrong with him."

Heat rose to her cheeks. "I've been worried sick," she said. "How was the trip?"

"Later," he said, his voice low and husky. "Right now I want to dance with you."

Suddenly feeling light and carefree, she floated into his arms. "I'm so glad you're home." She pressed her head against his chest.

"I couldn't stand you up. Now could I?"

Another twinge pinched at Cassidy's back. She stiffened.

Dell held her slightly away from him, his concerned gaze roving her face. "Everything okay?"

"Oh, I'm fine," she reassured him. "But I would feel better if I sat."

"Let's get you off your feet, then." He led her gently to a chair. "Can I get you anything?"

"A glass of punch would be nice. Thank you."

"Be right back."

As he made his way toward the refreshment table, Cassidy scanned the room, looking for each of her children. Sam again danced with Camilla. Emily and Jack played together with a small gathering of children, and Luke stood in a corner with a group of boys his own age. She continued her survey of the room and frowned. Where was Tarah?

Cassidy's eyes riveted to the door just as the girl slipped outside behind someone. Johnny!

Anger boiled inside of Cassidy. Was she being played for a fool? Tarah must have been seeing him all along!

She glanced back to the refreshment table. Dell was deep in conversation with the doctor. Well, she wasn't going to wait and give Johnny a chance to paw her daughter! Lumbering to her feet, Cassidy grabbed her coat and scarf.

An icy gust caught the door just as she opened it. Stepping outside, she gasped at the intensity of the cold. The ground was slippery as she made her way carefully down the steps, eyes scanning the area for Tarah and Johnny.

Please show me where they are, Lord.

The sound of angry voices caught her ears, and she cautiously moved toward the sound. Tarah and Johnny stood beside Dell's horse.

"You are not going to steal from my pa!" Tarah said hotly.

Johnny's voice came back smooth as freshly churned butter. "I told you, we're not stealing it from him. As soon as we get to Oregon and get settled in, we'll start paying him back."

"Why don't we just wait until we have the money, then? I just don't feel right going about it this way."

"I told you, Hon. It's the only way. Your pa'd skin me alive if he knew I was in love with his daughter."

"Oh, Johnny. . ."

The sound of rapture in Tarah's voice made Cassidy bristle. How dare he play on that child's emotions! Without thought, she stepped forward. "Johnny Cooper, I thought I told you to stay away from my daughter!"

"Cassidy," Tarah groaned.

Cassidy whirled around and pointed a finger at Tarah. "And to think I believed you when you told me you wouldn't see him anymore."

There was no defiance in Tarah's face. "I'm sorry, Cassidy, but I love him. We're getting married."

Rage boiled inside of Cassidy. "Over my dead, cold body are you marrying the likes of that vermin."

"Cassidy," Johnny broke in, amusement edging his voice, "I'm crushed." In his hand he held Dell's brown leather wallet.

"What do you think you are doing with my husband's money?"

"Now don't get riled up. I'm just taking it to the ranch for him."

She squinted, sizing him up. "Uh-huh, we'll see. Come, Tarah," she said firmly. "I think it's time your father knew about this relationship. I never should have kept it from him to begin with."

"Please, don't." Tears glistened in the violet eyes as Tarah pleaded.

"I'm sorry, but you've left me no choice." Cassidy lifted her skirt and turned.

Tarah gave a sharp intake of breath. "What do you think you are doing?"

Cassidy turned in time to see Johnny's pistol raised above her.

"Johnny, no!" Tarah screamed.

Pain exploded in Cassidy's head, and blackness claimed her.

❧

Dell frowned and glanced around the small room. Cassidy was nowhere to be seen. He motioned Sam from the dance floor.

"What's wrong, Pa?"

"Have you seen your ma?"

Sam shook his head. "Maybe she went to the. . ."

"I don't think so. She's been gone awhile." He grabbed his coat. "Just to be sure, I'll go out and check. You gather up the rest of the kids and ask if any of them has seen her."

Dell returned to the schoolhouse a moment later after confirming Cassidy wasn't in the privy outside. The children were gathered around, concern written plainly on their faces.

"Where's Tarah?" he asked.

Luke shrugged. "I saw her go outside with Johnny awhile ago."

"Johnny Cooper?" Dell asked with a frown. "What would she be doing with him? Besides, I told Johnny to take the supplies home." Anxiety gnawed at his stomach. "Stay here," he ordered.

Dell grabbed his saddlebag from its hook on the wall and opened the flap.

Feeling around for his gun, he frowned. His wallet, carrying the money they'd brought back from the sale of the stock, was missing.

"That no good, thieving. . ." So he had been right not to trust Johnny. He kicked himself mentally. He should have gone with his gut instinct in the first place. Taking his holster from the bag, he slid it around his hips and buckled it into place. There were more important things than money, right now. But he'd deal with Johnny once Cassidy and Tarah were safe. Slinging his saddlebag over his shoulder, he hurried into the frigid winter night.

His gaze scanned the schoolyard. Spying something lying a few feet away, he moved toward the object. Cassidy's scarf lay on the ground. As he bent to pick it up, he stared in horror. Drops of blood, crimson against the white of the snow, spotted the area.

Cassidy! Oh, God, no. Please, no.

Panicked, he ran back inside.

"What's wrong, Pa?" Sam asked.

Dell grabbed the boy's arm and led him away from the rest of the children. "I found this outside," he said, holding up the scarf. "And there was blood on the ground beside it."

"We gotta find her, Pa! What do you think happened?"

"I'm not sure, but it looks like Johnny took her and Tarah." Dell swiped a hand across his forehead. "What I can't figure out is why he'd do it. If he just wanted to steal the money from the sale, he could've done that."

"It was Tarah, Pa," Sam said hesitantly. "She told me awhile back they were going to be married as soon as she was of age."

Rage clouded Dell's senses as Sam went on. "Cassidy must have caught them together."

Dell shook his head, still unable to put it all together. All he knew was that he had to find Cassidy and Tarah.

"Sam, I'm going to unhitch one of the horses from the sleigh so I can go after your ma and sister. I want you to be extra careful and take the children home."

"I want to come with you, Pa."

Dell placed a hand on Sam's shoulder. "I know you do, Son. But I need you to look after the children for me. Can I count on you?"

"Yes, Sir."

"All right, then. I'll be home as soon as I find them."

"Everything okay, here?"

Dr. Simpson stood before him.

"My wife and daughter are missing." Dell showed him the scarf. "I found this outside on the ground, along with some blood. I'm going after them."

Doc frowned. "You need another man to ride along?"

"I sure could use you," Dell said. "I think my ranch foreman may have kidnaped them."

"Let me get my bag and tell my wife I'm coming with you," he said."

"Thanks. Do you have a saddle horse?"

Doc nodded. "I had a patient to see before I came, so I rode here."

"Good. I'll meet you out front."

By the time Dell loaded the children into the sleigh and sent them off toward home, Dr. Simpson was ready to ride.

"Let's take a moment to pray," the doctor suggested.

"I thought you were a doctor, not a preacher," Dell said gruffly, mounting his horse.

"I am. But I think prayer is in order right about now." He looked sharply at Dell. "I wouldn't want to ride off without His help if it were my wife and daughter out there in danger."

"You're right. Pray as we ride."

They set off in the direction of the tracks made by the sleigh that carried the supplies Dell had brought back from Abilene. The doctor said a quick but fervent prayer.

Dell had to admit he felt better after he echoed Simpson's amen. "They can't have gotten very far, with that sleigh loaded down with supplies," he said, speaking more for his own comfort than to reassure the doctor.

"We'll be able to cover more ground on horseback than he will with the sleigh and two women," the doctor said.

Dell nodded. *Oh, God, let them be safe.*

❧

Pain overwhelmed Cassidy as she came to. She tried to sit up but thought better of the idea as a wave of dizziness washed over her. She glanced up at the stars speeding by overhead.

"Cassidy, thank God you're awake." Tarah's tear-filled eyes gazed down at her.

"What happened?"

"Johnny knocked you out so you wouldn't go tell Pa."

"And you still came with him?"

"I wasn't going to, but he pulled his gun on me." Large tears rolled down her face.

Cassidy placed her hand on Tarah's arm. "I'm sorry, Sweetheart."

"You were right about him all along."

A gasp escaped Cassidy's mouth as a pain hit her back and crept around to the front.

"What's wrong?"

"I–I'm not sure," Cassidy said through gritted teeth as the pain held on then gradually subsided. "I think I might be getting ready to have the baby."

The blood drained from Tarah's face. "But it's too early."

"I know," she grimaced.

"Johnny Cooper, you turn around and take us home right this minute," Tarah called from the back of the sleigh where she sat with Cassidy's head on her lap. "My ma is about to have her baby."

"Shut up," he growled. "I don't have time to worry about a baby. We'll drop her off at the next town."

"If you think I'm going anywhere with you now, you have another think coming!"

"You'll do as you're told unless you want me to drop Cassidy off right now and let her freeze to death."

"I don't know how I could have ever thought I was in love with you."

"Little girl, I don't care if you're in love with me or not, but you're coming with me to make sure I get where I want to go." He turned and eyed her sternly. "Now sit down and be quiet before I gag you."

She turned and looked back down at Cassidy, fear clouding her eyes.

"God will take care of us," Cassidy comforted.

Tarah looked up and a hand flew to her throat. "I think He just did," she whispered.

"What is it?" Cassidy asked.

Tarah cast a furtive glance at Johnny's back and dipped her head closer. "Pa's coming."

"What do you mean?"

"He's behind us."

Relief flooded Cassidy's heart. God was in control, and Dell was coming to rescue her. She closed her eyes as a defense against the pain that seized her.

Hurry, Dell.

thirteen

Dell saw the sleigh speeding along the ice directly ahead of them. He drew his Colt pistol and kicked his horse to spur it on.

"Johnny, stop!" he yelled.

Johnny turned in the seat and whipped the reins hard. The horses sped up. Still, Dell and the doctor closed the distance easily, each going to one side of the sleigh. Dell leveled his pistol at Johnny's head.

"Stop the horses," he ordered.

"You wouldn't shoot me," Johnny hollered back over the pounding of the horses' hooves. "Not with your wife and daughter in back."

"Pull over now," Dell said through gritted teeth, "and I might not kill you."

Fear crossed Johnny's features.

"Look, I'm going to follow you wherever you're headed," Dell said. "And the longer you keep my wife and daughter in this freezing cold weather, the madder I'm going to get. I suggest you pull over right now."

Uncertainty flickered in Johnny's eyes. Seeming to weigh the odds of getting away, he pulled on the reins, gradually slowing the horses to a walk, then a full stop. Dell slipped his Colt back into its holster and jumped from his horse before Johnny could unholster his own gun. He grabbed Johnny's coat and dragged him from the sleigh, then drew back his fist.

"Dell," Cassidy's quiet voice broke through his rage. "Don't hurt him. Let him go."

"Let him go?" He blinked hard.

The doctor glanced up from beside Cassidy. "Better do as she says, Dell. You're about to be a father again."

Dell's grip loosened, and Johnny tumbled to the ground.

The baby was coming now? "It's too early," he groaned. "Just when I was starting to believe God wouldn't do it, it's about to happen again."

"What are you talking about?" the doctor asked, a frown furrowing his brow. "She's a few weeks early, but if we get her to a warm place, everything should be fine."

Dell turned to Johnny. "Get out of here and don't show your face in these parts ever again. It's a good thing for you that my wife is about to have that baby. Otherwise I'd tear you limb from limb."

"I won't make it to the next town without a horse," Johnny whined.

"I don't care," Dell growled.

Johnny shrank back.

"You can't leave him out here in this weather with no horse, Dell." Again Cassidy's pain-filled voice brought him to his senses.

"Take mine and go."

Not waiting to be told twice, Johnny moved toward the horse, eyeing Dell warily as he walked past him.

"Wait, Johnny!" called Tarah. "Give my pa his money."

Dell had forgotten about the money. Mentally, he kicked himself for not thinking to bring the sheriff along. He fingered his Colt and stared hard at Johnny as the scoundrel hesitated.

Finally he shrugged and reached into his coat. He grabbed the leather wallet and tossed it to the ground. Dell loosened his grip on his pistol

Tarah stomped forward and retrieved it from the snow. Glancing inside, she gave a grudging nod. "The money's there, Pa."

"What'd you expect?" Johnny mounted the horse quickly and grabbed the reins. "I didn't exactly have time to spend any of it." He glanced down at Tarah with an insolent grin. "It's too bad you didn't want to come with me, Hon. You and me would've had some good times together."

Dell clenched his fists and started toward him, but Johnny dug his spurs into the horse's flanks and rode away at a gallop.

From the sleigh, Cassidy moaned. Shaking himself from the anger still raging inside him, Dell went quickly to her side. "Is she all right, Doc?"

"She has a nasty cut, but I can tend to that," the man said, pressing a clean handkerchief to Cassidy's head. "What concerns me most is that her pains are coming pretty close together. Let's get her home before we have to deliver this baby in the cold."

Dell tied the doctor's horse to the back of the sleigh and settled into the seat. Tarah climbed up beside him. He flapped the reins, turning toward home.

"I'm sorry, Pa," she said, laying her head against his shoulder.

In spite of himself, Dell tensed at her touch. "I don't understand how you could go behind my back like this."

Her shoulders shook as she wept against him. "I believed him when he said he loved me," she said between large gulps of air. "Cassidy tried to warn me, but I wouldn't listen."

"Cassidy knew and didn't say anything?" He felt betrayed.

"Don't blame her. I promised I wouldn't have anything more to do with him, and she believed me." She lifted her head from his shoulder and sobbed into her hands. "I couldn't bear it if I cause more problems between you and Ma."

At the sound of "ma" on his daughter's lips, Dell's heart softened. "It's all right, Sweetheart. I'm not angry with Cassidy." He pulled a handkerchief from his breast pocket and offered it to the weeping girl. "I'm just relieved you're both all right. Now let's get her home."

❧

Cassidy was barely aware that they'd arrived home, so intense was the pain.

Dell lifted her gently into his arms and carried her inside.

"How is she?" Ellen asked. Four pairs of anxious eyes peered at Cassidy, waiting for the answer.

"I'm fine," Cassidy said, not wanting to alarm any of the children.

"The baby's coming." Dell's answer was clipped. "Fill a basin with water and grab some clean linen."

Once inside the bedroom, he laid her gently on the bed and began to undress her.

"How are you, Darling?" he asked.

Cassidy winced. "My head hurts."

Dell glanced down at the pillow and a groan escaped his lips. "It's bleeding."

"Johnny knocked me out."

Something akin to a roar emitted from deep inside Dell. "If I had known that, I would have killed him."

"I know." Another contraction gripped her, and she squeezed Dell's hand to ward off the pain.

"Doc!" Dell yelled.

"Wait. Get me into my nightgown first." Modesty was too embedded in Cassidy for her to allow even a doctor to see her unclad.

When she was wearing a fresh nightgown, he called the doctor in. Dell cleared his throat and backed toward the door. "Well, I, uh. . ."

"Don't leave me," Cassidy implored, catching his hesitant gaze. She reached for him.

"I–I don't know if I can. . ."

Cassidy knew what he meant. The memories of Anna's death during childbirth were too deep, and he was consumed with fear. She couldn't stop a moan as the next wave of pain seized her.

Dell was back at her side in a flash.

"You're—staying—with—me," she insisted through gritted teeth, digging her nails into his arm.

"That okay, Doc?"

"As long as you keep out of the way."

Dr. Simpson checked her contractions and pressed on her belly. "Everything seems to be right on track," he announced.

"Won't be long now."

"Oh, God, Oh, God, please!" Dell said from her bedside.

Irritation rose up inside of Cassidy. "Dell!" she bellowed through the pain. "Be quiet! And don't you dare pass out on me like you did at the wedding!"

The doctor's eyebrows shot up, and a rumble of laughter shook his shoulders.

"Don't cross a woman in labor, Dell," he said, moving to check the cut on Cassidy's head. "It's not bad," he mumbled as though to himself. "The bleeding's stopped for the most part."

"Is it wrong for a man to worry about his wife?" Dell asked, looking to the doctor for affirmation.

"Yes!" Cassidy exclaimed.

"First you complain that I don't give you enough attention, and now you want me to stop caring?" he growled.

Dr. Simpson looked up from bandaging Cassidy's head. "Uh, this might not be the proper time to—"

"This is the perfect time," Cassidy interjected. "It's the only time I can get him still long enough to talk."

"Why is it wrong for a man to want his wife to live?" Dell directed the question to the doctor, but it was Cassidy who answered.

"I don't know why Anna was taken from you and the children," she said, her voice still sharp from pain and frustration. "But I have no intention of dying. God willing, I'll live to care for my children until I hold my grandchildren, and possibly my great-grandchildren in my arms."

He winced as she squeezed his hand again. When the contraction was over, she continued as though she had never been interrupted. "You have to stop living your life in fear, dwelling on the past."

"My faith isn't as strong as yours, Cass. I can't bear the thought of losing you."

"Women have babies—they have all through the ages. Sometimes they die, and sometimes they don't. Look at me, Dell."

His tortured gaze met hers, and her heart went out to him.

"There are more ways to lose a person than for that person to die," she said pointedly.

His eyes narrowed. "You saying you're going to leave me?"

"Of course not! I could never hurt God and the children that way. Besides, I love you. But this unreasonable fear you have is causing a wedge between us whether you want it to or not."

Her body went rigid as another pain seized her. She clamped her lips tight, trying not to cry out. Would this pain ever stop?

"It's almost time for you to start pushing, Mrs. St. John. You might want to hold the rest of this fascinating conversation until your babies are delivered."

Did he say babies? Must be the pain affecting her hearing.

"Dell, listen to me."

He leaned in closer, tears misting his eyes. "You—have—to—" She let out a deep groan and tears stung her eyes. "You have to let go of your fear and trust God."

"Cassidy," he moaned. "Please don't try to talk, Darling. Save your strength."

Cassidy shook her head. "You have to hear this. I have faith in God that He'll watch me and keep me safe. And when it's time for me to go to be with Him, He'll take me. But I'll tell you this much." She was starting to get riled again. "Whether I live or die has nothing whatsoever to do with you and any silly bargain you made with God! Just how much power do you think you have over a person's life?"

"Okay, I see a head," the doctor announced. "Push with the next contraction."

Another pain squeezed her body, and Cassidy bore down, pushing with all her might.

"Rest a minute," the doctor ordered.

She lay back, exhausted. "If—I—can—trust—God—to—care—for—me—can't—you?" she asked, panting between each word.

He pressed her hand to his lips, wiping her sweat-soaked brow with his handkerchief. "I'll try, my darling."

"Get ready to push again," Dr. Simpson ordered.

Summoning her strength, Cassidy pushed once more, the pain nearly overwhelming her senses. Again and again she obeyed the doctor's orders, until at last, a small, but healthy infant made its way into the world.

Dell peeked over Cassidy to the baby. "It's a girl," he cried, tears streaming down his handsome face.

Tears filled Cassidy's eyes. "I told you it would be," she said, managing a smug, little smile.

Their infant daughter let out a wail.

"I was right, too. Didn't I tell you she'd take after you?" Dell said with a teasing grin.

Another pain gripped Cassidy's body. "Something's wrong."

"What do you mean?" A look of terror crossed Dell's face.

"I–I feel another pain coming."

"That would be baby number two." Dr. Simpson placed the freshly wrapped infant in Dell's arms.

Cassidy would have laughed if the pain hadn't been so intense. Twins. She'd asked God for a child, and He'd given her twins. The tears spilled over onto her cheeks. How good He was.

"All right, Mrs. St. John, are you ready to do this again?" the doctor asked.

"I'm ready," she said through gritted teeth.

Within moments their second baby arrived—a boy, crying lustily as he entered the world. Soon the doctor had him wrapped and placed in Dell's other arm.

Tears streamed down Dell's face as he looked at Cassidy. "Do you want to see them?"

"Of course. Sit on the bed next to me."

"Only for a moment," the doctor warned. "We need to make sure they stay warm."

Cassidy looked at her red, squalling babies and knew she had never seen or heard anything so beautiful in her life.

"Oh, Dell. Isn't God wonderful?"

His tearful gaze captured hers, and he nodded. A thrill passed over Cassidy's heart. She knew her husband was a man who had just had a change of heart.

They heard a quiet tap at the door.

"Open the door," Dell called. "My hands are full."

It was Ellen. "I thought I heard two babies crying."

"You did." Dell replied.

"Oh my. Do you need some help, Doctor?"

"I could use someone to bathe the twins while I finish with their ma. Take them to the front room where the fire is. And make sure they're wrapped tightly after their bath so they don't lose any body heat."

Ellen nodded, then glanced at Dell. "Carry them into the sitting room for me. I'll get Tarah to help."

❧

By the time the doctor was finished tending to Cassidy and Ellen had changed the bedding, a beaming Dell had returned with the babies. He lay one on each side of her. She nuzzled first one, then the other, and sighed with contentment.

"Well, I think my work here is done," Dr. Simpson said. "I must say, this has been the most interesting birth of my career." He looked pointedly at the new parents. "And the most enlightening."

"Sorry, Doc," Dell muttered.

The man placed a firm hand on Dell's shoulder. "Your wife is a smart woman—and most definitely still alive. Do you both a favor and stop being a fool."

Cassidy giggled as Dell blinked in surprise at the candid remark.

"Life and death are in the hand of the Almighty. Even we doctors, much as we'd like to take credit, can't control what God ordains." He zipped his leather bag and lifted it from the dresser. "Now I suggest you stop trying to control how He does His business and relax."

He turned, lifted the latch on the door, and opened it.

"Besides," he said with a grin, "your wife is a strong woman, most likely capable of bearing a dozen children."

A gasp escaped Cassidy's lips. A dozen children.

The doctor lifted his hand and exited the room.

"Well, I guess he gave me what for, didn't he?" Dell asked with a wry grin.

"You needed to hear it."

"I suppose. . ." Dell glanced at the sleeping babies. "What are you going to name them?" he asked.

"I don't know. How about if you name the boy and I name the girl?"

"Sounds reasonable." Dell squinted, obviously deep in thought. "How about Timothy?"

Cassidy wrinkled her nose.

"Matthew?"

"No."

"I thought you said I get to name the boy." Dell's eyes twinkled, and a smile spread over his face.

"Okay, I won't say anything about the next one you pick."

"Hiram," he said with a smirk.

"This beautiful little boy does not look like a—"

Dell threw back his head and laughed heartily. "All right. What do you want to call him?"

Cassidy eyed him. "Can I still name the girl?"

He gave her a wry grin. "I guess."

"All right. Let's call him William, after my brother. It'll mean so much to Emily."

Dell nodded. "Sounds like a pretty good name. Mind if I call him Will?"

"That's fine. But not Willie or Billy. My brother hated those nicknames."

"What about our sweet little girl, here?" he asked, cooing at his daughter, whose tiny hand wrapped around his finger.

"I'd like to call her Hope."

Bending over, he brushed Cassidy's forehead with his lips. "Hope and Will. Our babies." He gently unwrapped Hope's fingers from his. "Do you feel up to seeing the rest of the children for a few minutes? They're sort of waiting outside the door."

"Of course."

Dell went to the door and opened it to reveal five excited faces.

Slowly, they filed in, one by one, kissing Cassidy on the cheek and running gentle hands over the fuzzy baby heads of their new sister and brother.

Tarah stood before Cassidy with trembling lips. "Forgive me?" was all she could manage before a fresh onslaught of tears.

"Of course I forgive you, Sweetheart. I'm just glad everything worked out the way it did." Cassidy grinned at her. "I imagine you'll pay penance enough helping me take care of two babies!"

"Oh, Ma, I truly love you." Tarah maneuvered cautiously around the twins and gave Cassidy a squeeze.

Cassidy's heart leaped from the wonder of it all. God knew what it took to finally make them a family. She stroked Tarah's ebony hair. "I truly love you, too."

"All right," Dell said with authority. "Everyone out. Your ma needs her rest."

The children lifted their voices in protest. But Dell was firm. "You'll have plenty of time to see her and the babies tomorrow, but for now I want you in your beds. No arguments."

They didn't have to be told again, and one by one they slowly left the room.

"Now as for you, my darling," he said. "I want you to get some rest, too."

"I will. I feel like I could sleep for a month."

Dell chuckled. "You'll be lucky to get a couple hours before one or both want to be fed."

"Then you'd better let me sleep."

He pulled the covers up around her, careful not cover the babies' heads.

"Cassidy, I want you to know I thought about what you said earlier." He reached forward and brushed a damp strand of hair away from her eyes. "About trusting God to care for you."

"Yes?"

"And I think I'm beginning to understand. Anna was tiny and weak from the start. But you. . .you're so strong—strong enough to argue with me the whole time you were having the babies."

"Well, you're so thick-headed," she said in her own defense. "And I was feeling pretty cranky."

"I can imagine," he drawled. "And Doc had a point about me trying to control whether someone lives or dies."

Hope rose in Cassidy's heart. "That's entirely up to God."

"I'm beginning to realize that. Anyway, like the doctor said, you're a very strong woman and could most likely bear a dozen children."

"Dell!" Cassidy gasped.

"Don't worry," he said softly. "I don't intend to have a dozen more. But I wouldn't mind another one or two, eventually."

Cassidy stared up at him, eyes wide. "Do you mean you want a real marriage?"

He nodded. "I've allowed fear of losing you to control our relationship. But not anymore."

"Not anymore?" Cassidy repeated, tears welling up in her eyes.

"Nope. Never again."

Cassidy's pulse quickened as his gaze melted into hers. Gently, he lowered his head inch by inch until their lips met. His hands went to either side of her neck as he deepened the kiss. When he finally released her, tears glistened in his blue eyes. "I love you more than anything in this world, Cassidy St. John." Lovingly, he stroked her cheek. "I'll make it all up to you. I promise."

Cassidy shook her head. "I just want to go forward. There's

been too much looking back in this family—too much trying to pay for the past."

"All right," Dell said softly. "There'll be no more talk of the past, then. We start fresh right now."

"What about God?" Cassidy asked. "Our marriage will never be the way it is supposed to be unless we make Him the center of our lives."

"I reckon it's time to start fresh with Him, too."

Cassidy saw the mist in his eyes and smiled. "Behold all things become new," she said wearily, just before a yawn rose from inside of her, catching her unaware.

With his forefinger, Dell gently traced a line from her cheekbone to her chin. "I want you to get some rest while you can," he said softly. "I'll be here on a pallet if you need me for anything."

"Oh, Dell, don't sleep on the floor," Cassidy protested.

He smiled tenderly. "I've spent enough nights alone. From now on, I'm sleeping wherever you are."

After dropping a final kiss on her upturned lips, he blew out the lamp.

Cassidy pressed a kiss to each little head beside her, then snuggled down under the covers. Her mouth curved into a smile as she drifted to sleep.

A Letter To Our Readers

Dear Reader:

In order that we might better contribute to your reading enjoyment, we would appreciate your taking a few minutes to respond to the following questions. We welcome your comments and read each form and letter we receive. When completed, please return to the following:

Rebecca Germany, Fiction Editor
Heartsong Presents
PO Box 719
Uhrichsville, Ohio 44683

1. Did you enjoy reading *Darling Cassidy* by Tracey Victoria Bateman?

    ❏ Very much! I would like to see more books by this author!

    ❏ Moderately. I would have enjoyed it more if

_____

_____

2. Are you a member of **Heartsong Presents**? Yes ❏ No ❏
If no, where did you purchase this book?_____

_____

3. How would you rate, on a scale from 1 (poor) to 5 (superior), the cover design?_____

4. On a scale from 1 (poor) to 10 (superior), please rate the following elements.

_____ Heroine   _____ Plot

_____ Hero   _____ Inspirational theme

_____ Setting   _____ Secondary characters

5. These characters were special because _____

_____

_____

6. How has this book inspired your life? _____

_____

_____

7. What settings would you like to see covered in future
   Heartsong Presents books? _____

_____

_____

8. What are some inspirational themes you would like to see
   treated in future books? _____

_____

_____

9. Would you be interested in reading other **Heartsong
   Presents** titles?   Yes ☐   No ☐

10. Please check your age range:
    ☐ Under 18   ☐ 18-24   ☐ 25-34
    ☐ 35-45   ☐ 46-55   ☐ Over 55

11. How many hours per week do you read? _____

Name _____

Occupation _____

Address _____

City _____ State _____ Zip _____

·······Presents·······

Great Inspirational Romance at a Great Price!

Heartsong Presents books are inspirational romances in contemporary and historical settings, designed to give you an enjoyable, spirit-lifting reading experience. You can choose wonderfully written titles from some of today's best authors like Peggy Darty, Sally Laity, Tracie Peterson, Colleen L. Reece, Lauraine Snelling, and many others.

When ordering quantities less than twelve, above titles are $2.95 each.
Not all titles may be available at time of order.
